Cold Winter Rain

Other Books By Steven P. Gregory

The Dreamer's Mistress And Other Stories (2012)

Cold Winter Rain

By

Steven P. Gregory

Cold Winter Rain

Oak Mountain Press, LLC

Birmingham, Alabama

ISBN-10: 0985992816

EAN-13: 9780985992811

In the long run, we are all dead.

—JOHN MAYNARD KEYNES

OAK MOUNTAIN PRESS

This book is dedicated to Jan, my wife and editor, and Sam, my son and cover artist.

CHAPTER ONE

Saturday January 21

Don Kramer's face looked like he'd shaved it with a rasp every morning for the last thirty years.

"Hear you're good," Kramer said.

The voice matched the face.

"You hear that," I said.

Kramer sat on the other side of my desk in the client chair. He wore a dark gray pinstripe suit and held a wet gray trench coat in one hand.

Except for a week's worth of scattered dry days, the rain hadn't stopped since the new year began. Kramer dropped the trench coat beside the chair, where it shed a puddle of rainwater onto the floor.

"What can I do for you?" I asked.

"Find my daughter." Kramer pulled a three-by-five color print out of the pocket of his suit coat, leaned across the desk, and laid it in front of me. "Kristina."

1

A tall blonde girl of about eighteen looked out of the picture from in front of a soccer goal. The print was the kind you can have done at a copy store.

"Pretty girl," I said. "How long has she been missing?"

"Two days," Kramer said. He tugged a pack of cigarettes out of his inside coat pocket and lit one.

People don't usually smoke in my office, but the man's daughter was missing. He took a long drag and held the cigarette commando style, the tip shielded in his hand.

"Anyone else trying to find her?"

"Birmingham cops. Alabama state cops. Jefferson County. FBI." He snorted. "Alabama Southern cops, too, if you want to count them. I don't."

Kramer smoked and stared hard at me. I said nothing.

The raw January wind blew harder against the clapboard siding of the building, a damp gust sweeping more rain in sheets across the Gulf of Mexico.

Looking past the bar just outside my office door and the ten tables on the deck, I could see the dark gray water of the Gulf, surf running to whitecaps past the sand bar two hundred yards out, and beyond, a necklace of lighted natural gas derricks.

I went around the desk and out to the bar, selected a bottle of Early Times, brought it and two glasses back to the desk and poured two drinks. "Sorry I don't have any single malt scotch."

Kramer swallowed the whiskey in one gulp and set the glass down easy. "Thanks for the drink. I've had worse. You going to help me?"

I took a sip of the bourbon. It was warm going down. Smoky. The warmth spread seductively across my midsection.

"The obvious question here is, why do you need me? Police, state police, feds – what can I do that they can't?"

Kramer took out another cigarette. "You can do what I asked you to do when I walked in here. Find my daughter. She's missing two days. I want her found. Now."

I picked up the picture again. "Was an Amber Alert issued?"

"She's nineteen. Amber Alerts are issued only if the child is seventeen or younger. Media are all over it though. Satellite trucks outside the house, police press conferences."

I nodded. "Where was she last seen?"

"You going to help me?"

"Maybe. Maybe not. I need facts. If she's run away from a husband, the answer is no. I don't do that kind of work."

"Fuck," Kramer said. He stubbed out the cigarette on the bottom of his wingtip. "There's no goddamn husband. The girl is nineteen years old. She's a college kid. She's a good girl."

He gestured toward the picture. "Soccer scholarship. English major. Her mother and I. . . ."

His voice trailed off and he looked away. "She's our only girl. I want her found, goddamn it. I'll pay your top rate. You want a retainer? You want cash? Tell me how much."

"One thousand dollars a day plus expenses. But I don't need a retainer. I'll send you a bill."

"I've been paid more than that for an hour. You're hired."

Kramer lit another cigarette. "Keep the photo. But I want you to come back to Birmingham with me this afternoon. Meet my wife. Susan. She was the last family member to speak to Kris. I've got a friend's private jet waiting for me at Brookley Field."

I walked around to the front of the desk, half sat on the corner. "All right. But I make my own travel arrangements. If we arrived in Birmingham late this afternoon, I could not get much done tonight. I'll fly up tomorrow. I'll meet with you and your wife in the morning."

I stood. "And there's one other thing. If I find your daughter and she doesn't want to come with me, I'll let you know where she is, but whether she returns to home and hearth is her decision."

I held out my hand. "Deal?"

He cocked his head to the side for minute, appraising, then stood. "Deal. Work it however you want to, Slate. Just find her." Kramer held out one finger. "Kris's full name is Kristina Alexandra Kramer." He shrugged. "Susan majored in Russian at Middlebury, worked at the U.S. embassy in Moscow a couple of years after college."

"I'll do my best. Tell me your address in Birmingham."

Kramer gave me the address, shook my hand, and walked out of the office, out of the bar, and into the cold rain.

3

* * *

Don Kramer may not have remembered me, but I remembered him.

Two decades ago, when I was in law school, I clerked for six weeks one summer in the office of the attorney general of Alabama. Kramer worked as a special assistant AG for three years during the benighted Guy Hunt's term as governor. Kramer was only five years out of law school himself then.

Kramer had served in a Special Forces unit in El Salvador, and the AG had recruited him to lead an investigation and prosecution of some crooks from New Orleans who'd sold fraudulent oil leases to Alabama investors.

The national press picked up the story, and Kramer's picture ended up on the cover of *The Wall Street Journal*.

Kramer had been a tough prosecutor but no politician. Word had it he'd made a deal with the professional politicians not to run for office.

In return, Kramer got to spend three years kicking ass and taking names, and some heavy-duty bad guys went to jail for a long time.

I picked up my drink, walked around the bar and sat at a table next to the window overlooking the beach, and, beyond, the Gulf of Mexico.

As far down the beach in either direction as I could see, there was not a single human being.

After a device called a blowout preventer had failed, on the bottom of the sea floor five thousand feet down and a little over one hundred miles south-southwest of where I sat, to prevent a blowout, the next eighteen months had been a slow, tough slog for every business on the Gulf. Barring any more oil spills from the new well Washington had given BP permission to drill, by late May, there wouldn't be a place to lay a beach towel flat for a half mile east or west.

I had spent a good part of November, December, and January repairing a year's worth of wear and tear on my little beach bar. Pressure-treated pine lumber that will take twenty years of outdoor exposure as part of the hardscape of a suburban inland home will survive maybe three years of ninety per cent humidity, salt spray, wind-driven grit, and coastal sun reflected off sand as white as refined sugar.

Teak would probably have lasted as long as the Gulf coast, or at least until the next category three hurricane, but late each fall when I considered the cost of rebuilding with rare lumber imported from another continent, I defaulted to yellow pine from the local lumber yard.

The thirty-by-fifty foot deck overlooking the Gulf had benefited from the annual application of time and money. The new wood was already fading to a soft gray. By Memorial Day, the new parts of the deck would be indistinguishable from the old.

The rain had diminished, falling now in a wind-driven sprinkle. At the shoreline fifty yards east, a small group of sandpipers, resembling quail in their wind-ruffled feather coats, made desultory rushes at the receding water.

My bartenders and waitresses had January and February off. Across the jetty that allowed seawater to flow in and out of Big Lagoon, the Pink Pony Pub kept a bartender and a waitress or two on hand all winter. My bar was never quite as busy except for the month or two after the school year ended and before the hottest part of summer.

I opened the place up and aired it out most days. A handyman friend, who lived with a tattoo artist in a mobile home in Foley and worked up and down the coast in the winter on beach property restoration, dropped in from time to time to do a little sanding, varnishing, and light carpentry.

The truth was I didn't have much more to do than any other beach bum in the middle of winter in lower Alabama.

I looked at the print of Kristina Kramer her father had left on my desk. What did she have to tell me?

I finished my drink without taking my eyes off the picture, then walked around to the bar and washed and dried my glass and Kramer's and placed them in the rack.

Back in my office, I removed the Glock in its shoulder holster from the top desk drawer and threw the rig on. I pulled my rain parka off the coat rack, put the picture of Kris Kramer in the inside pocket, and walked in the rain to my car.

Kramer's problem would stay with me for a while, and there was nothing I could do but embrace it.

By five, the rain had stopped. In the cabin of the *Anna Grace*, I dug my suitcase out from under my bed and threw in socks and underwear and a couple of changes of clothes and a vinyl zipper bag I kept packed with essentials: razor, toothbrush, dental floss, a full box of Federal Hydra-Shok in forty-five caliber.

CHAPTER TWO

Sunday January 22

The grinder on the programmable coffee maker in the galley switched on at six twenty-five a.m. It sounded like a blender filled with rocks. After a few seconds, the smell of freshly-brewed coffee filled the cabin.

I pulled on sweats and made a glass of sugar-free Tang from the dwindling supply I'd bought when Kraft discontinued it. I drank the glass off in one go, then poured a cup of coffee and went up on deck.

The sun wasn't up, but the incandescent bulbs strapped to the top of every other catwalk support pole around the marina made enough light to see by. The air was damp and cold, heavy with the smells of diesel fuel and stale salt water and fish, and in the quiet morning, I could hear water lapping rhythmically against pilings and the resting hulls of boats.

I sipped the coffee and wondered what had happened to Kris Kramer. She didn't look to be the kind of kid who'd just run away from her family. But then, that description probably fit lots of runaways.

I'd probably find her. I just hoped she was still alive when I did.

I finished the coffee, went below deck, and swapped the sweats for a pair of tights, running shorts, and a black hoodie. I carried my shoes out on deck and laced them by the fresh pink light of false dawn.

I stepped onto the catwalk, walked out of the marina to the bay road, and started to run.

I ran slowly, shuffling along at about a nine-minute pace.

My neighbors along the canal were stirring, a couple of fishing boats, a forty-foot Bertram and a smaller Hatteras convertible already backing out of their slips, navigation lights glowing red and green, diesel engines growling and snorting in the cool morning air. Preparing for their long early runs to offshore fishing grounds, coordinates already programmed into GPS-guided navigation systems, men moved purposefully along the decks. At my feet, damp patches of asphalt remained from yesterday's rain.

I jogged three miles out to the highway, my condensing breaths following me like watery spirits, then turned back, walking the last half mile before the marina.

Back on the *Anna Grace,* I put a blueberry bagel in the toaster oven and showered and shaved while it heated.

Out of the head, I dressed in a hurry. My heaviest khakis, a burgundy plaid flannel shirt, beige cotton sweater, suede hiking boots.

I cut the bagel and smeared cream cheese on one side, put the pieces back together and wrapped the bagel in a paper towel. I heated milk in the microwave, poured a measure into a thermos with two aspartame tablets, and filled the thermos with coffee.

I opened the locker beside my bunk and pulled out the Bianchi shoulder rig, the Glock 36 heavy in the holster. I strapped on the rig, threw a couple of changes of clothing and some underwear into a soft carryon, and slipped my Mac Air and its charger into the backpack where I stowed my flight gear.

I checked email on my iPhone. Nothing but spam. The phone clicked into its hard case and the package clipped onto my belt.

I threw on a lined navy parka, locked the door of the cabin and stepped off the boat and onto the dock. One thing about living on a boat. One step and you're away from home.

There were few travelers on the beach road. I gazed at the Lounge as it went by in the driver's window of the Toyota. The place would still be there when I got back. I had a feeling it might be a while.

Out of habit, or inertia, or sentiment, or stubbornness or, maybe, stupidity, I'd held onto the Toyota Camry I'd been driving the day Anna and David were killed.

I'd had the old rice burner re-painted in the original beige and had a rebuilt engine, flywheel and clutch installed at two hundred eighty thousand miles.

The original flywheel had acquired chipped teeth after about a hundred fifty-thousand miles. Every ten starts or so, I'd have to open the door, put my left foot on the ground and rock the car before the starter pinion would engage.

I'd driven it the last fifty thousand miles with a blown head gasket and a rear main seal that leaked oil like a dripping faucet.

The odometer on the Toyota read 339053 as I turned north onto Highway 59 for Jack Edwards airport.

Automobiles are all pretty much the same unless you believe the Madison Avenue hype. They have running gear and four wheels, they have seats bolted to an integral body and frame, some glass and curved metal and paint and carpet and plastic, or leather if you pay more, to make them look like something besides machines. Oddly, they are, along with aircraft and, perhaps, toasters, one of the few technologies that have come down to the twenty-first century virtually unchanged, except for cosmetics and fluff and some federally-mandated safety gear, since nineteen fifty-five.

And automobiles, whether German or Japanese or U.S. or Swedish, all go fast enough to kill you. Even with a seat belt.

Of course, if all else failed, there was the air bag – the law of unintended consequences. What was the government's air bag score so far? Ten dead kids and three petite women for every fat, stupid insurance salesman saved?

At the airport I opened the security gate with my card key and parked outside my little metal T-hangar. I untied my airplane and waited while the attendant pulled it out of the hangar with a tow cart. I stepped onto the wing, opened the canopy, and swung in the duffel that held my flight gear. I pulled out the rudder lock and reached behind the seat for a paper towel and the fuel drain, climbed down and began the preflight.

I climbed the two steps up into the cockpit of the Albatros, ratcheting the built-in step back into its receptacle as I went, strapped in, and ran through the start checklist.

When I was done flipping switches, I started up the Sapphire unit and listened to it whine up to idle speed. Twenty seconds later, I pushed the engine start button and moved the throttle to the start position.

The little Ivchenko AI-25TL turbofan engine came to life with a low moan. At stable engine idle, the Sapphire starter unit cut off. Its engine whistling now, the plane was almost ready to fly.

I closed and latched the plexiglass canopy and watched the gauges in front of me while the operating temps climbed into green. I called Mobile Departure for my IFR clearance, taxied out to the hold-short line for runway two-four, and called out my intentions on one-two-two point eight.

The rising sun illuminated the eastern sky in pink and orange. Looking over my left shoulder to check to see if some lazy or stupid pilot was bumbling down final without calling out his position, I eased onto the runway, lined up, and moved the throttle smoothly to the stop.

The jet paused for a moment while the engine's hot section swallowed the slug of kerosene and air. Then the heavy turbine wheels spooled up, and the seatback shoved me in the back and kept shoving.

In three seconds, we were airborne.

I keyed the mike and called Mobile approach on one-one-eight point five. "Approach, Experimental November Seven Five Eight Mike Sierra off Gulf Shores for Birmingham, IFR, through two thousand for five thousand."

"Eight Mike Sierra, approach, radar contact, turn right heading zero-one-zero, climb and maintain seven thousand."

Thirty minutes later I was being vectored to the ILS for runway five in Birmingham. I lowered the gear and flaps and held a hundred knots on final. A few raindrops splattered on the windshield.

I kept the localizer and glideslope centered, mostly out of habit, since the runway appeared in and out of the mist, and below fifteen hundred feet the mist cleared.

The tires chirp-chirped onto the runway, and I taxied to the FBO and shut down. They had a rental agency Ford Taurus – synonymous for rental car – waiting for me.

I drove the Taurus, the wipers sweeping every few seconds, out Airport Road past Forest Hill Cemetery and the chop shops and auto detailers, juked over to Second Avenue North, crossed under the Red Mountain Expressway and into downtown.

CHAPTER THREE

The Tutwiler Hotel occupied a renovated former apartment building a block from the Jefferson County courthouse.

Clad in red brick in understated Beaux-Arts style, the seven-story building, according to a plaque near the front door, was listed in the National Register of Historic Places. The lobby was trimmed in brass, mahogany, and white marble with black veins. Working fireplaces heated some of the rooms in winter.

Kramer called me on my cell phone while I was checking in. "Slate. Are you in town?"

"Yes," I said.

"Where?"

"The Tutwiler."

"I'm at my office. You're just down the street. I'll be there in five minutes. Meet me in the dining room."

"I haven't checked in yet," I said, but he was gone.

I booked the room for a week, sent my bags ahead, and walked down to the dining room. I refused a menu and told the maitre d' I was waiting for someone.

Kramer walked into the dining room through the outside entrance two minutes after I'd entered. He was in a charcoal plaid suit with a yellow tie, and he was carrying a black document case.

"Coffee," Kramer said to the waiter before he sat down.

Kramer looked around. Only a couple of other morning diners remained in the dining room, and they were seated under another window fifty feet away.

The waiter brought coffee for Kramer and retreated.

"You're probably going to speak to the Birmingham police, campus cops. I'll give you the FBI agents' names, too. Cops do what cops do. They want to do this the traditional way. The cop way. Interview friends, try to figure out a boyfriend angle or a family feud. But my daughter's disappearance is not about her."

"Then what is it about?"

"Kris didn't have the kinds of problems in her life that lead to a runaway or an angry boyfriend. She didn't hang out in bars or do any of the other stupid things that get girls, get young women her age in trouble."

Kramer leaned forward, intense but in control. "I think it's related to a legal matter I've been on."

"I see. What sort of legal matter?"

Kramer took a slug of coffee. He was not a big guy – I had him by an inch of height and probably twenty pounds – but in his hard, calloused hands the china cup looked as delicate as a thimble.

"I'm not able, sitting here right now, to tell you as much as you probably need to know."

"Privilege?"

"Yes. And even more."

"What do you mean?"

"Having this information could be dangerous."

"Danger is an occupational hazard."

Kramer nodded slightly and looked around. Fifty feet away, the waiter was putting out silverware for the lunch buffet.

"This goes back a long way, Slate. All the way back to when I was in the AG's office."

"I knew you were in Montgomery for some time."

"You were a clerk when I was there."

I was a little surprised but didn't show it. Yesterday Kramer had made no indication that he remembered me.

"Yeah, I remember you," he said, and for a second I thought I'd spoken the thought aloud.

"You worked hard and kept your mouth shut. Most non-lawyers and too many lawyers think talking is the only skill a lawyer needs. There's an aphorism: 'An empty vessel makes the most noise.' When I asked around, your name came up. I figured you still remembered that it's easier to learn something with your mouth shut."

Some people might not agree, but I nodded.

Kramer pointed to the document case. "There are some things I can show you and some I can't. These are my copies of documents from the oil lease cases I worked on when I was with the office of the Attorney General. They're old and most of the information is public anyway. I could tell you what you need to know, but we'd be here all day, and I've got other people to see. It's faster if you read, and you need the background. There's a memo to the file and an index. The index is new. But start with the memo."

"Sounds good. But what's this got to do with your daughter's disappearance?"

"My daughter – Kris did the index for me during her Christmas break."

"Kris was working for you?"

Kramer threw down the rest of his coffee. "Just some clerical stuff during vacations, sometimes on weekends. But she's smart. Learned a lot. Knew a lot."

"Do you think she's been kidnapped?"

Kramer was silent. Then: "That's a reasonable assumption, don't you think?"

"But there's been no contact, no demands. Right?"

"That's correct."

"And it's been – what – three days now. I'm sure you know that's a long time to go by without a ransom demand."

"These are not ordinary kidnappers."

Kramer stood. "Got somewhere to be. Meeting my wife and son at church. Read the file. You're involved because, if I'm right and Kris's disappearance stems from my work, I can't share all my work with every goddamned three-letter agency with a 202 area code. I don't remember giving you copies of the memo and index. They might be subject to the work product privilege, probably not the attorney-client. Hell. You're a lawyer, anyway. Finish reviewing the documents today and tonight. You need to meet my wife and my son Paul at my house in the morning. Try to make it around seven-thirty."

And he was gone.

In my hotel room I sat in a burgundy fabric armchair near the window overlooking a parking lot, opened the document case, and pulled out the memorandum.

The memo began with the standard SUBJECT/TO/FROM/DATE heading. Written three months earlier, the memorandum was addressed to the Minerals Investigation file and to "DRK" – Don Kramer. No pride of authorship had driven this document; the "FROM" line was blank. The memo began with an introduction and background including a quotation from an obscure journal of geology:

Citronelle Oil Field, Mobile County, Alabama
Everett Eaves
AAPG Special Volumes
Volume M 24: North American Oil and Gas Fields, Pages 259 - 275 (1976)

The Citronelle field was discovered in 1955 by the Zack Brooks Drilling Company No. 1 Donovan, SW 1/4, NW 1/4, Sec. 25, T2N, R3W, Mobile County, Alabama. The well produced from the lower Glen Rose Formation at a depth of 10,879 ft (3,315.9

m). During the next 10 years, 434 productive wells were drilled. The productive limits completely enveloped the town of Citronelle, 32 mi (51.5 km) north of Mobile, Alabama. Forty-acre spacing, low gas-oil ratio, and rapid bottomhole-pressure drop, necessitating pumping of all wells, resulted in slow and spasmodic development. Unitization of 139 wells for waterflood was initiated in 1961, and a saltwater-injection program proved successful. Later, fresh water from the Wilcox Formation was used for injection fluids. By May 1966 all wells were unitized, and on December 31, 1973, the field had produced over 107 million bbl of oil.

The memorandum continued with an overview of the oil and gas business in Alabama:

The discovery of the Citronelle field in what is called the Glen Rose Formation focused attention on the potential for oil and gas development in southwest Alabama. Today, the extent of the oil reservoir off the coast of Alabama, due south of Citronelle, is well known. One-fourth of U.S. oil production now flows out of the Gulf of Mexico. In the late 1970s, large deposits of natural gas were discovered underneath the sea floor off the Alabama Gulf Coast. Alabama ranks ninth out of the fifty states in natural gas production and tenth in proven reserves. The retail value of the petroleum produced onshore and off exceeds $1.2 billion dollars annually. Alabama receives almost $300 million annually in the form of lease bonuses, royalties, trust-fund investment income, and severance taxes.

Moreover, the Gulf of Mexico is perhaps the only part of the continental United States where new substantial petroleum deposits could remain to be discovered. As late as 1999, British Petroleum drilled a discovery well 25,770 feet deep 155 statute miles due south of the Mississippi coastline in what geologists call the Mississippi Canyon and found the largest petroleum field in the

Gulf. Petroleum geologists estimate that this field (originally named Crazy Horse but now for the sake of political correctness called the Thunder Horse oil field), contains one to three billion barrels of oil.

I didn't know the details about the discovery well or the Citronelle field, but to say the least, BP had become a household name, and during the summer of 2010, the *nom du jour* on cable TV and Facebook and in the Twitterverse.

Some substantial but unknown portion of that three billion barrels had flowed into the Gulf of Mexico from a broken pipe at the bottom of the sea below BP's collapsed Deepwater Horizon drilling rig.

A few brown spots of it had ended up on the beach sand below my bar.

I had spent too much time at the Alabama Gulf Coast not to understand the back story for the file Kramer had left with me. At night the platforms out in the Gulf resembled large fishing boats at anchor.

But I was curious about the missing attribution for the author. One thing I knew: Kramer was not the author. I knew the man to be a thorough lawyer who would have demanded and appreciated the kind of work that someone had put into the introduction, but as a lawyer, Kramer was no scholar.

As a lawyer, Kramer was a killer. Figuratively speaking.

I skimmed the remainder of the memorandum and returned it to its place in the document case. Kris Kramer's index was next. I laid the index on the table and called room service to order a sandwich and a pot of coffee.

Reviewing these files reminded me of law practice. I couldn't help thinking I should be recording my time, noting "Review file" in the billing software. I'd have plenty to record this afternoon. I had a lot to learn, and I settled in to read.

By three I had reviewed half the documents and had made a few notes on a legal pad someone had left in the document case, perhaps for me, but more likely because lawyers leave legal pads everywhere.

First, these documents related only tangentially, if at all, to the oil lease cases Kramer had prosecuted twenty years earlier. Those cases were securities swindles where some crooks from New Orleans sold partnerships on properties in Texas and Oklahoma that had never existed. Assessments, legal opinions, all the pieces of paper had been in place, but the deals were wholly fraudulent.

The documents in Kramer's document case instead related to an ongoing, present-day legal matter.

Kramer and the Woolf firm were investigating information they had learned from two independent sources about underreporting, or underrecording, of gas and oil pump volumes by small independent production companies operating in several sites in Alabama, all south of Birmingham.

Gas and oil leases were priced based on volume, and underreporting these volumes and thereby shortchanging landowners on lease revenues had generated lawsuits since someone thought to drill a well where oil seeped out of the ground.

Recording production volume remained to this day in the hands of the production companies, not the landowners, and the temptation to cheat proved difficult to resist.

The file looked interesting enough from a plaintiff's lawyer's perspective; more than one potential class action suggested itself, though the size of the alleged losses would not rival the Bernie Madoff scandal.

Such cases were grist-of-the-mill civil litigation. Similar lawsuits were probably pending in every state with working oil and gas wells, and I could see little that should make anyone desperate enough to kidnap the daughter of a lawyer.

And why had Kramer told me these files related to the work he'd done a generation ago?

But then I reached a subsection of the file containing information a little outside the workaday findings of a law firm preparing to represent a client in a business dispute. One dark brown folder, the type with a ribbon that could be tied for security, was marked Confidential – Qui Tam.

Inside the folder were the usual files marked Drafts, Notes, Research, as well as a thin tan envelope marked Client Information. The envelope was sealed, and, redundantly, bore the legend SEALED in heavy black marker.

So I opened the envelope with my lockblade knife.

Inside were eleven pages of handwritten notes on yellow legal paper. Nothing else. The notes began with a name and address: Michael Godchaux, 123 Royal Street, New Orleans, Louisiana. A cell phone number and email address followed.

After this information the word Relator appeared, underscored twice. The notes described a pattern of bribery and corruption in the operation of oil and gas wells on state lands in the State of Alabama which, if true, not only would support a cause of action in a *qui tam* lawsuit but might also implicate current and past holders of constitutional offices in Alabama in criminal activity.

No link between the name Michael Godchaux and the information about wrongdoing appeared in the notes. Godchaux's address provided the only hint of any connection to Kramer's oil lease cases from years before.

I memorized the telephone number. Some facts are better left out of the electronic memories of computers or cell phones. Memorizing numbers is something I can do, though I have no idea why or how. Names of people, not so much. Numbers, like music, have a rhythm that names rarely manage.

Qui tam. The Latin words literally mean "who comes."

Historically, kings and lesser rulers in Europe from time to time would set aside a day or a few days when they would allow any subject a private audience for the purpose of offering evidence that someone entrusted with the property of the crown was stealing. "Who comes" before the king?

Today *qui tam* litigation is often initiated by an employee who becomes aware that her employer, a defense contractor, or a pharmaceutical company, or a healthcare provider, is violating federal law, or is overcharging the Department of Defense or Medicare. Such lawsuits have gained in popularity among plaintiffs' lawyers as tort reform legislation and rulings in federal courts have shrunk the envelope of viable class action litigation.

Qui tam complaints are filed under seal to protect the identity of the plaintiff, who is called the relator. After the complaint is filed, the government agency alleged to be cheated by the defendant is notified and provided the opportunity to take over the litigation.

The relator receives fifteen per cent of any funds the government collects.

The eleven pages of notes included information about numerous small operators of oil and gas companies, employees of those entities, and state employees.

The notes also set out dates and times when representatives of these entities had meetings scheduled in the state capital with two lobbyists and with the attorney general and governor of Alabama.

No wonder these notes were maintained in a sealed file. If the information in the notes were true, the relator here might be eligible for the federal witness protection program.

The Birmingham Public Library, a modern glass building of seven stories, stood directly across Richard Arrington Boulevard from the hotel. After sifting through files for six hours, I needed a break.

Before leaving the room, I placed the eleven pages of handwritten notes back in their folder, and, on an impulse, placed them in the room safe. The information could be valuable or even dangerous, and someone had taken the precaution of sealing the envelope. A little security seemed reasonable.

I took the stairs down to the hotel lobby, crossed the street, entered the library through the glass doors, and weaved my way past the bums and winos pretending to be respectable street people hanging out in the atrium.

The library's escalator carried me to the reference room on the third floor.

The librarian at the desk, a tall, skinny guy with granny glasses and a ponytail going gray, fetched volume 1 of the current *Martindale-Hubbell Law Directory* out of a back room. I gave him my driver's license, signed a card, and carried the three-pound book to the nearest table.

Martindale-Hubbell, in its many volumes, lists lawyers in the United States and most other countries by name, date of birth, college and law school attended, location, law firm, and type of practice. The information in the book was available online, but I'd spent enough time in the hotel room, and no one hacks into eyes on paper.

For the law firms that buy subscriptions – most of them – *Martindale* includes a description of the law firm's practice and a mini-resumé for each lawyer in the firm.

Other volumes contain precise and detailed descriptions of the law of each listed jurisdiction – contracts, corporations, procedure, criminal law. Compiling the outlines is a prestigious assignment for a law firm.

Volume 1 contained listings for Alabama, Alaska, Arizona, and Arkansas.

Kramer's law firm kept its offices downtown at Park Plaza, a glass and concrete office tower overlooking Linn Park, Birmingham's courthouse square. The firm's entry listed around fifty lawyers. William Francis Woolf was the managing partner.

Woolf was fifty-five, a Tulane Law School graduate. The Woolf in the firm's name appeared to be William's father, one of the founders of the firm, now retired or deceased.

The office building was only two blocks away. I could walk down there tomorrow and drop in unannounced to see my client. I knew much less at this point than he did about Kris's disappearance, and neither of us seemed to know much about her whereabouts. I had more documents to review.

I closed the heavy book and returned it to the John Lennon wannabe at the desk and walked out of the library and across the street to the hotel. Back in the room I called room service and ordered a turkey sandwich and two cups of coffee. After they arrived, I settled in to read.

At seven I took a break to turn on the room's flat-screen TV monitor and find a cable news channel. Kramer had told me the case had attracted media interest, and I knew that after the media frenzy surrounding the young woman from Mountain Brook who'd disappeared in Aruba in 2005, another missing young blonde woman from Birmingham would be irresistible to the piranhas of sensationalism who pass for today's journalists.

I was not disappointed. One network featured a wolfish graying man who called himself a psychiatrist and specialized in diagnoses of crime victims and perpetrators he'd never met and never would meet. Another cable news platform offered a fat bleached blonde who alternated between gushing sentimentality and a practiced sneer at every comment offered by her guests, all of whom seemed to be either lawyers or psychologists. Disgusted and a little ashamed, I hit the Power button and went back to the documents.

It was still raining when I finished the last folder a few minutes before midnight. I closed the file, threw my zabuton on the floor, and sat for ten minutes. Then I undressed, took a quick shower, and lay down to a sleep without dreams.

CHAPTER FOUR

Monday January 23

When I woke up at four-thirty and pulled apart the curtains at the window, I could see light rain streaking past the streetlights in front of the hotel.

By five I was in the hotel's small exercise room. I warmed up on a Schwinn Airdyne and then did a hundred sit-ups and three sets of reps on eight stations on the Universal machine. By six I was showered, shaved, and dressed, and I went down to the hotel dining room and ordered two scrambled eggs, toast, and coffee. I ate in ten minutes and went back upstairs to finish preparing for the day.

I called Kramer around seven. He answered his cell before I heard a ringtone. "Slate. Come on out now. You know where we are?" He recited the address. "FBI is due here any minute. You may as well say hello to them. I'm sure they'll be happy to meet you." The sarcasm dripped from his voice.

Kramer lived in Mountain Brook, a wealthy enclave of hills and sub-urban forest a few minutes southeast of the city. The exterior of the house was stucco and brick, with timbered eaves, in what might be called English Arts & Crafts in a real estate brochure.

Across the street from the Kramer home, a CNN satellite truck and a truck from the local NBC TV station were illegally parked. I left the rental car in the driveway behind a black Ford sedan that could have worn a vanity tag with the initials FBI. I walked up the wet brick path and rang the front doorbell. My arrival did not launch any investigative journalists from their dry seats in the satellite trucks. I didn't blame them. I wouldn't get out in the weather for me either.

A thin boy about fifteen with acne and black hair in bangs so long they covered his eyes answered. I introduced myself, and he asked me to step inside the foyer. He closed the door.

"I'm Paul Kramer," the boy said. "My father told me you would be here this morning. I'll go and tell him you're here."

I waited less than a minute. Kramer bounded through the archway leading from a hall that appeared to provide access to the other rooms of the main floor. "Slate," he said. "Glad you're here early. FBI wants to talk to my son Paul right now, so it's a good time to meet Susan. Come on back."

Kramer led me through the hall and into a large kitchen with a central island encircled by barstools. In a nook at one end of the kitchen stood a massive leather and walnut booth worthy of a private club.

A woman with ash blonde hair, her face as smooth and unlined as a ten-year-old's, sat on one of the barstools. She wore a black jogging suit with some sort of gold fabric belt. A heavy gold crucifix hung between her breasts. Her feet were bare except for black tennis footies. I wondered if I should have taken off my shoes before entering the house, but I noticed that Kramer was wearing his wingtips. Lawyers' shoes.

If Susan Kramer was her husband's age, she had engaged the services of an excellent plastic surgeon. Or maybe it was heredity. Or good bones.

"Slate," Kramer was saying. "This is my wife. Susan. Susan, meet Mr. Slate. Mr. Slate has agreed to help us find Kris."

"I see," Susan Kramer said. She didn't stand or offer her hand.

"Slate is here to help us, Susan."

"I'm sorry. I don't mean to be rude. But FBI agents are here in the house. They have the resources of the government at their disposal. I trust them. I trust the police. And I place my ultimate trust in the power of prayer and in the power of miracles and in the Blessed Virgin. I just don't see. . . ."

"No." Kramer cut her off. "No, you don't see."

"Now who's being rude?"

"Folks, maybe this is a bad time. I can come back later."

"No, Slate," Kramer said. "Susan, I've watched this man's career. He's a smart lawyer, and now he takes on situations like ours. I've seen the FBI screw up too many kidnapping cases. The two members of my law school class who joined the FBI could not have gotten a job in the county DA's office. I've hired him, and he stays."

Susan Kramer stood and said, "I'll be upstairs. Father Kelly is waiting in the salon. We will pray together. It was nice to meet you, Mr. Slate."

"Whatever," Kramer muttered to her retreating back. "Sorry, Slate. Susan handles stress with anger and sessions with the priest. And I'm the one with high blood pressure. Let's go in the library. Maybe the fibbies are finished interviewing Paul."

One room on the front of Kramer's house jutted past the remainder of the house's facade. Floor-to-ceiling bookshelves covered one wall. An antique writing desk of dark wood with painted Oriental figures sat under the double windows facing the street. Paul Kramer sat near the bookshelves in a wing chair covered in solid red fabric. Facing the boy, the two FBI agents, a man and a woman, occupied the ends of a couch covered in a red fabric that appeared to be silk.

Kramer walked in and stood over the couch. I hung back near the door. "Not finished yet?" Kramer asked the room in general.

"Almost." The female FBI agent glanced up at Kramer. "Paul was just telling us about going with his mother to pick up Kris from school."

"And that's all I can remember," the boy said. "May I go now?"

"Yes," Kramer and the female agent said simultaneously. Paul got up, and the two agents both stood and shook the boy's hand. He nodded to me as he walked past.

"Agent William Alston, Agent Patricia Sanders, meet Mr. Slate. Mr. Slate is a lawyer, and I've hired him to help with the effort to locate Kris."

The two FBI agents turned toward me as I followed Kramer to the center of the room. Both had been issued straight from the twenty-first-century federal law enforcement handbook. The man, Alston, about six-three, 205. Dark thinning gray-blond hair, trim, cheap suit, black cap toe shoes with thick soles. Probably an ex-jock. The woman, Sanders, probably five-seven, 135, wore her brown hair shoulder-length and pulled back with a shell clasp. Dressed better than the man: dark blue suit, pink shirt, probably Brooks Brothers or Ann Taylor. Odd eyes: one green, one brown. Heterochromia iridium. Anna used to tell me I read too much.

I shook their hands in turn. "It's just Slate."

Agent Sanders nodded. "Slate, then. You were retained to advise the family on legal issues related to Kris Kramer's disappearance?"

Before I could answer, Kramer spoke. "The fact that Slate has been retained is not privileged. But any question as to the nature of any legal advice he may offer falls squarely within the privilege."

"And the fact that you find it necessary to retain counsel when your daughter is missing raises interesting issues," Sanders said.

"Well, I'm sure what Agent Sanders means is that it is a little unusual for a family with a missing child to hire counsel this early when law enforcement has no reason to suspect a family member might be involved," Alston said. He turned to Sanders. "I'm sure Mr. Kramer is just being thorough and careful, and after all, he is himself a well-respected attorney. Natural for him to retain counsel during any difficulty."

"Does your practice include criminal law, Attorney Slate?" Sanders asked.

"No," I said.

"Media law?"

"Nope."

"Domestic relations?"

"Missed again. Sorry. No more guesses. Three strikes."

"You're out," Bill Alston said.

Patricia Sanders rolled her eyes. "Why is it that the testosterone levels and the sports metaphors multiply geometrically when the number of men in a room increases arithmetically?" Sanders asked.

"That is a mathematical conundrum on par with Fermat's Last Theorem," I said.

"Well. Way too much of both in here for me," Sanders said. "I'm going upstairs to speak with Mrs. Kramer."

"She's with the priest," Alston reminded her.

"Good. I'll speak with him too. We'll take all the help we can get."

Don Kramer and Agent Alston spent the next fifteen minutes explaining the avenues of investigation they were pursuing: speaking with Kris's friends and teachers, interviewing her family, reviewing posts on social media. The FBI treated all such disappearances as possible kidnappings until proven wrong, but so far no communications from kidnappers had surfaced.

Agent Sanders' footsteps on the stairs prompted Alston to check his watch and to suggest that it was time for them to head back downtown. Sanders and Alston shook Kramer's hand. Alston clapped him on the shoulder. I followed them into the hall. Kramer opened the door for the agents; they looked back, nodded to me, and walked out into the rain. One media cameraman in bright red rain gear hustled out of his van and filmed them getting into their government sedan and driving away. That footage would make for scintillating television.

Kramer led me back into the library. "I apologize for Susan earlier," he said. "She'll come around. She always does. She just has to understand things are moving too fast for me to consult with her every thirty seconds."

"Not a problem," I said. "But I do need to speak with her about that afternoon when she picked Kris up at school. So I hope she comes around soon."

"Count on it," Kramer said. "How's the reading going? Draw any conclusions?"

"It's clearly a good lawsuit. But most good lawsuits don't drive defendants to commit criminal acts before they're filed. What makes this one different?"

"It's different because one defendant, or group of defendants, is the New Orleans Mob." Kramer nodded. "Same bunch twenty years later. Meet the new boss. Same as the old boss."

After the meeting with Kramer, I spoke briefly with Paul Kramer about the afternoon he'd last seen his sister. That conversation revealed nothing useful. Kramer gave me a little more background on the relator in the *qui tam* matter and why he'd placed the notes in a sealed envelope. I returned to the hotel, spent the afternoon reviewing my notes and reading the file, and ate a passable dinner of broiled red snapper and steamed vegetables downstairs in the hotel restaurant.

CHAPTER FIVE

Tuesday, January 24

By midnight the rain had slowed to a drizzle. The streets of the city were wet, and in the weak light from the streetlights three stories down from my hotel room, they looked almost clean.

I took the little bronze Buddha out of my suitcase and placed it on the nightstand, lit a stick of incense, unrolled my zabuton, placed my bolster in the center, and just sat, astride the bolster in seiza posture, for fifteen minutes. Thoughts came, and I acknowledged them, then allowed them to float away.

For a year after the accident, when I meditated, all the images and thoughts floating up to consciousness were of Anna or David, their faces, a phrase, how they moved and breathed; or sometimes of twisted metal and smoking airbags. Then an occasional thought of work or chores or a conversation with someone else would come. By now the mix of images and thoughts approached fifty-fifty.

I rolled off the bolster, stretched my stiff legs, then tossed the bolster and the mat onto a chair and went to bed.

At two in the morning, my cell phone rang. I was in that half-sleep when dreams begin, and I lay still for a moment to let the jangle of the bell clear my head.

I answered on the sixth ring.

"Slate," the caller said.

"Yeah," I said.

"It's Grubbs. Not asleep, were you?"

"Of course not. I was evaluating my investment strategy for the transition to the renminbi as the world's reserve currency."

Leon Grubbs's little sister Tasha had worked for me at my old law firm as a paralegal in the early nineties. From eighty-three to eighty-five Grubbs had started at weakside linebacker at Grambling and made second-team All-Southern conference three consecutive times.

Grubbs had also majored in criminal justice and made academic All-American twice.

I knew a couple of people who'd seen Grubbs play football. Running backs didn't get to Grubbs' corner, and he didn't need support from the defensive backs. When Grubbs hit a ball carrier, the guy stayed hit.

Back home after school, Grubbs made one of the highest scores ever recorded on the Birmingham police entrance exam and rose up the ranks like an ebony rocket.

Eighteen months ago he'd made captain and the same day got appointed to his dream job, at least until he made chief – Deputy Chief of the Investigative Operations Bureau of the Birmingham Police Department. Chief of Detectives.

Middle-of-the-night calls from Leon Grubbs were not likely to convey good news. "What's up?" I said.

"You and me. I'm down in the railroad yard. Morris Avenue and Twenty-First. Not far from your hotel."

In the background I heard static from what could only be a police radio approach closer to Grubbs and his cell phone, then Grubbs' muffled voice mingled with more radio static and the voice of another man.

"Just a second," Grubbs said. The line went silent while I wondered how Grubbs knew I was in town.

When he came back on the line, he seemed to have heard my thought.

"Yeah, I know where you are. Get your butt down here now. I've got a murder victim in an expensive suit. He's carrying one of your business cards in his shirt pocket."

I told Grubbs I'd get there when I could, went into the bathroom, splashed cold water on my face, and rubbed the skin hard with a clean white towel.

I pulled on a red Marines sweatshirt and a rain suit with a hood, strapped on the Glock, and walked the six plus blocks in the cold rain down to the rail yards that divided the north side of Birmingham from the south side.

Most Birmingham citizens would have advised against that walk, but cold rain keeps the gangs indoors too. I could have driven the Taurus, but the walk in the cold wet air slowed my arrival, helped me think, and, mostly, woke me up.

Down past Morris Avenue between Twenty-first and Twenty-second Street North, a dozen cops moved slowly over and across the tracks, surrounded by four black-and-white units with blue lights turning, too bright in the semi-darkness of the city night, and one ambulance, the attendants sitting in the front seat out of the rain while the police did their work.

Grubbs was chewing on a wet cigar and talking to another detective and a couple of uniforms, their hats wrapped in plastic.

Grubbs finished with the uniforms before he cocked his head toward me and gestured with the cigar. "Come over here," he said.

I followed him across three railroad tracks, the wet iron rails glistening in the artificial light.

Grubbs was just over six feet, and even now, just shy of fifty, the shoulders and waist made a V. He looked like he could still shed the defensive end and nail the tailback.

But this was no night for games. A dark plastic tarp covered a shape that was unmistakably a body.

Grubbs motioned with his thumb. I bent over the tarp and lifted a corner near what appeared to be the head.

Kramer was on his back. The hair was soaking wet and plastered against the scalp. There was blood on the back of the head and a deep bruise on the left side of the face.

Raindrops fell steadily into the open sightless eyes, but the dead man didn't blink.

"Looks like a nine-millimeter in the back of the head," Grubbs said. "Know him?"

I eased the tarp back over the face and stood up. "His name was Kramer. Donald R. Kramer. He's – he was a lawyer here in Birmingham."

"Any idea why he was carrying your card?"

I shook my head. "Lots of lawyers have my cards."

Grubbs nodded. "Let's hope they don't all end up lying dead in the rain."

"Yeah," I said. "That would be good. Okay if I go back to bed now?"

Grubbs looked down the tracks for a minute as though he were thinking about taking the next train out of town. Finally, he turned back to me. "Sure," he said.

I turned and began stepping over the wasteland of wet tracks, careful to place my feet on the heavy dark cross ties.

"Oh, Slate," Grubbs called. "Call me if you remember anything about this Kramer. Got me?"

I waved without turning around. Grubbs was a guy who needed to have the last word.

At a quarter after six in the morning, running at about eight-minute pace, I was two miles down First Avenue, across the viaduct over the old Sloss Furnace, past the waterworks office with its perpetual wall of water, in a neighborhood of warehouses and wholesalers, heading in the general direction of the airport.

The morning air was cold and damp, last night's rainwater turning the asphalt streets into cold air humidifiers.

When I hit two and half miles, I crossed the street and headed back. Uphill now; I had to slow down.

I was not twenty anymore. And I didn't want to be.

Back at the hotel, I showered and changed into a white shirt with gray slacks, tasseled loafers, blue Brooks Brothers blazer and rep stripe tie.

I took the elevator down to the lobby, picked up a copy of the *Birmingham News* at the counter, pushed through the double doors of the hotel restaurant and ordered blueberry waffles, two eggs and coffee.

The shooting of my client was not mentioned in the paper, but at Alabama, recruiting seemed to be going well. Around here, people had their priorities straight.

I ate breakfast slowly and drank three cups of strong coffee. I needed the coffee. Sleep had eluded me after I returned to the hotel.

So far, I hadn't been paid, my client was dead, and I had no idea where to look for his missing daughter. This case was looking like a real winner.

The Homicide Division office on First Avenue North occupied the second floor of police headquarters.

Grubbs' personal space was an eight-by-ten glass cubicle in the corner overlooking a dozen cops' desks in a bullpen. Grubbs was sitting in there behind his desk.

Despite the fact that he'd been up investigating a homicide the night before, Grubbs appeared to have showered and shaved, and he was wearing a starched blue oxford-cloth shirt, a plaid tie, and pressed khakis.

He also wore a Colt's Government Model .45 semi-automatic pistol in a belt holster.

I tapped on the glass and opened the door. Grubbs nodded. "So what do you know about this Kramer?" he said.

"Good morning to you, too, Captain."

"Yeah, right. Pleasantries, et cetera. So what do you know? Were you working for him?"

"Not much and yes."

"The girl?"

I smiled a little. Pleasant. Innocent. "What girl, Captain?"

Grubbs lowered his eyes and slowly, almost imperceptibly, shook his head. "Not a good first inning for you, Slate."

"Captain. . . ."

Grubbs looked up. "Nobody likes a smart ass, Slate. Stop this 'Captain' shit and let's talk straight."

I leaned over the desk, palms flat on the corners, my eyes inches from the top of Grubbs' head.

"A client is dead. Last night you asked me to identify the body. As though you didn't already have him identified. This morning you ask about the girl. I agree with you. Let's talk straight. But maybe you should go first."

To his credit, Grubbs held still.

"All right, Slate," he said. "Point made. Now unless you intend to kiss the top of my nappy head, sit down over there and let's see if we can do each other any good."

I sat in the vinyl and chrome chair in the corner and folded my arms.

Grubbs said, "I assume, since he was your client, you know about Kramer."

I shrugged. "Lawyer. Downtown firm. Used to be assistant AG."

Grubbs shook his head. "You don't know much, Slate."

I heaved a sigh and sat forward, elbows on my knees.

"Kramer came to see me Saturday in Gulf Shores. We talked for ten, fifteen minutes. He hired me to look for his daughter. I visited the house yesterday and met his wife and two agents from the Bureau. I was planning to spend some more time with him and his wife today. What else should I know?"

"Nothing, considering it's you. No reason to expect much."

"You're right. I live on a boat and run a bar. You have the vast resources of the government at your disposal. What is it you shouldn't expect me to know?"

Grubbs shook his head again as though he were having trouble hearing. "You still planning to talk to Mrs. Kramer?"

I nodded. "Not a very good time, but I think I have to."

Grubbs nodded. "That would be my view."

He stood, came around the desk and opened the door. "I have a few more things to do before mid-morning. I'll pick you up at ten-thirty at your hotel. I'll tell you what I can on the way out to Mountain Brook."

I followed him out the door. "Isn't Mountain Brook out of your jurisdiction, Captain?"

Grubbs dismissed me with a flick of his hand. "We still make house calls," he said.

CHAPTER SIX

Building security at Park Plaza would not have met New York standards. The first time I visited a New York lawyer's office after 9-11, security in the building lobby outpaced the TSA at LaGuardia. But here, an elderly fellow in a green blazer with a nifty gold identification badge on the left breast pocket sat inside a circular cubicle a few steps from the revolving doors, reading the sports section of *The Tuscaloosa News*.

After I stood at the counter for a few seconds, he looked up reluctantly. "Help you?" he said.

"I think so. I'm looking for Woolf White Waldstein."

"They got three floors. Seventeen, eighteen, nineteen. Reception on seventeen. Take the elevator there," he pointed backwards with a thumb.

"Thanks." I smiled, tapped the counter for emphasis, just a regular Joe, another lawyer, another suit among the hundreds who came and went around his desk every day, trotting up to the main tenant's office with a Glock strapped under his arm and a lock-blade knife clipped to his right trouser pocket.

On the seventeenth floor, the elevator opened to a marble lobby with closed double doors on the right and a large reception area on the left. A brass and wood spiral staircase that must have cost more than the *Anna Grace* connected the law firm's two main floors.

In front and to the right of the stairs sat a blonde receptionist wearing a headset and a neon smile. She spoke into the headset and managed to continue that conversation while conveying attentiveness to me as though I were far more important than the caller.

Despite her efforts, it didn't look as though the call would end soon. I strolled over to the floor-to-ceiling windows overlooking the courthouse square and, beyond, the hills of North Birmingham.

"Sir? Sir, may I help you?"

I turned around. The receptionist had removed her headset and had taken a couple of steps in my direction. "Yes," I said. "My name is Slate. I'm here to see Mr. Woolf."

"Senior or Junior?"

"I didn't know both of them were still practicing," I said. "I'm here to see the Mr. Woolf who is the managing partner. Is he in this morning?"

"I can check with his assistant, sir. Did you have an appointment?"

"No." I shook my head. "No appointment."

"Well – and it's Mr. Slate? May I tell her your full name?"

"Just tell her Slate. I need to speak with Mr. Woolf about Don Kramer."

"Oh. Yes. I'm sorry sir. Just one moment." She replaced the headset and spoke into it. Thirty seconds later, a woman in her fifties, wearing a blue wool skirt, white blouse, and plaid pullover sweater, her white hair pulled into a tight chignon, materialized in the elevator lobby behind me. "Mr. Slate. Katherine Richards. Mr. Woolf's secretary. Follow me right this way, sir." She turned and we went through a door beside the elevators that opened with an electronic key pad into a corridor lined with filing cabinets and interspersed with secretarial workstations.

Woolf had the southwest corner office. The office was adequate for a managing partner of a fifty-lawyer firm, the cherry wood furniture slightly worn, solid but understated.

In one corner were stacked half a dozen file boxes with case names in black marker on the ends. A couple were open, and documents were half-pulled from some of the files. Legal pads filled with notes were lying on the floor in a pile next to the boxes.

It looked as though Woolf might be a real lawyer.

Woolf was standing behind his desk. He wore a white shirt with the sleeves rolled halfway to his elbows and a blue scroll-pattern tie pulled loose.

Woolf reached across the desk to shake my hand. It was not a stretch for him. He must have been six-seven and had arms to match.

"Mr. Slate, Bill Woolf. Ms. Richards told me you wanted to see me about Don Kramer. What is your interest in my law partner?"

"I met him last Saturday, and I identified his body for the police last night. I think you may want to spare me a couple of minutes."

Woolf didn't say a word. Just nodded a couple of times, looked me over for a second, walked over to close his office door, and returned to sit down behind his desk.

"Sit down," Woolf said. "Let's talk. I've got about fifteen minutes."

I sat in one of Woolf's leather client chairs and crossed my legs. The chairs were a little nicer than mine, but his desk lacked a view of the Gulf of Mexico.

Woolf leaned toward me, his elbows on the desk. "Why did the police call you?"

"They found my business card in your partner's shirt pocket."

Woolf nodded. "I see. So, I could ask, why was your business card in my law partner's pocket? But this is not a deposition, and you came to see me. So why don't you just tell me why you're here? If this is about money, I can tell you, I've never heard of you, so this law firm owes you nothing as far as I know."

Lawyers, especially litigators, experience more confrontations in the average week, just in the normal course of business, than the average person does in a lifetime. Most lawyers are comfortable with confrontation, and some learn to seek it out, to initiate it, some because they learn to need it, others because they see it as the shortest way through life.

Woolf, I figured, was in the short-way-through group. Sometimes, so was I. "I don't need your money, and I never heard of you before yesterday either."

"Fair enough, Slate. So why are you here?"

"But I had heard of Don Kramer before he came to see me in Gulf Shores. He brought this."

I laid the picture of Kris Kramer on the desk in front of Woolf.

"She's missing, and he asked me to find her. Now he's dead, but I intend to do what he asked me to do. That's why I'm here."

Woolf looked down at the picture of Kris Kramer and nodded several times as though he had confirmed something.

"Do you have a business card?" he asked.

I placed a card on the desk beside the picture.

Woolf glanced at the card, looked up at me and nodded again. "All right. What do you want to know?"

"Did Kramer talk to you about Kris's disappearance?"

"A little, yeah. I knew he was going to see a new investigator he'd heard about from one of his law enforcement contacts. I knew he was going to Baldwin County, so that must have been you. He was frustrated with the local police, especially the campus cops. Not sure why; I would assume they couldn't find water in the river."

"Do you think the girl's disappearance and Kramer's murder could be connected?"

Woolf shrugged. "Who knows? Kramer was working night and day trying to find her. We relieved him of all his duties here. If you knew Kramer or his reputation, you would know he'd charge hell with a bucket of ice water if he thought it would help bring Kris back. Maybe he had arranged an exchange with the kidnappers and it went badly."

"Is that what you think happened?"

"Again, Mr. Slate, I just do not know."

"What was Kramer working on before she disappeared?"

Woolf leaned away from the desk and crossed his fingers behind his head. "Well, that. I don't think I can speak with you about legal matters the firm may be handling. Sorry. Our clients are off limits. Privilege."

I nodded. "Right. But still, it's possible, isn't it? Was Kramer working on any cases where he was getting any threats, any matters with criminal involvement?"

"Can't tell you, Mr. Slate. Won't tell you. Our clients expect their business to remain privileged. It's one of my jobs to see it stays that way."

"Does the name Godchaux mean anything to you? Michael Godchaux of New Orleans?"

Woolf shook his head slowly. "No. I don't think so. But if it's a witness or even a client, I would not necessarily have known details about what Kramer was working on, and even if I did, I could neither confirm nor deny that the name means anything to me."

Woolf's face was absolutely blank. He probably played poker well.

I stood. "Well, I hoped this would be more helpful."

I picked up the photograph and gestured at the card. "Call if you think of anything that might be useful."

He was already out of his chair and showing me to the door. He had me by seven inches. I hate having to look up at people.

"I wish I could help," he said. "I'd like to see Kris safe and sound, too. Known her since she was a baby. Let me know if there's anything I can do. Except opening client files of course."

"I'll see myself out," I said. I was saying that too much, lately.

CHAPTER SEVEN

The sky was still gray and overcast, and the temperature was in the mid-40s. Cold when it's damp.

Leon Grubbs picked me up at the rear entrance of the hotel in a black Ford LTD without markings. There was a portable blue light suction-cupped to the dashboard and a stubby antenna on the back window. We took Twentieth Street headed south. At least Grubbs let me sit up front.

"I miss the old cop antennas," I told Grubbs after I got in and fastened the seat belt.

"You miss what?"

"You know, the old cop antennas. You knew for sure that black Ford sedan was a police car when you saw one of those twelve-foot whips tied down to the bumper."

"Hmmph. Progress, Slate. I've heard some cops in the big cities even know how to turn on a computer now."

At the Fifth Avenue intersection, Grubbs turned left. At the end of the block, he pulled up to the fire hydrant and handed me a five.

"Safari Coffee," he said.

I looked down at the money.

"Right there on the corner."

I didn't move.

"So I'm addicted," he said. "Go in and get two coffees. For me, tall regular coffee, skim milk, one Equal."

I got out of the car without taking the bill.

"Your money's no good here," I said.

I could smell the coffee from the sidewalk. In a corner near the front window sat a polished brass coffee roaster. The place was decorated in a jungle theme and featured Kenya AA dark roast. There was a line, and I didn't have a badge to show. Grubbs would have waited too. He might park on the hydrant, but he wouldn't cut in front of a line of citizens.

I paid for the coffee, mixed in the milk and sweetener at a little bar in the corner, and snapped plastic lids on the cups.

Grubbs drove north on Twenty-first Street and then took Abraham Woods Boulevard past Linn Park and the Birmingham Museum of Art and down to the cloverleaf onto Highway 280 East.

I tore the little strip off the plastic top and sipped the coffee. It wasn't just good and strong. It was good and hot.

"So how did you know?" I said.

"Know what?"

"When you called my cell phone just after midnight, you said you were not far from my hotel."

Grubbs inclined his head an inch.

"So how'd you know I was there?"

Grubbs glanced at me, then back to the street. "I'm a trained detective," he said. "But, Slate, tell me something I don't know, for once. Did Kramer tell you whether he'd been contacted by anyone holding his daughter? Kidnappers? Could he have been making a ransom drop without telling anyone?"

"He told me there had been no contact. And if he was making a ransom drop, he didn't tell me."

Grubbs nodded and drove in silence.

In spite of the cold and the damp air, shoppers were rolling into the parking lot at Brookwood Mall in their Mercedes and Jaguars and Range Rovers, suburban women in leggings and leather jackets and Hermes scarves ready for a tough day hitting the spa, a boutique clothing store, an Oriental rug dealer.

Mountain Brook was Alabama's toniest suburb, a spiderweb of hilly residential streets connected loosely at three hubs called "villages" by the locals. In the "villages," – English Village, Mountain Brook Village, and Crestline – just Crestline to the locals, no "Village" – there were hair and nail salons, specialty groceries, trendy bars and bake shops, and investment managers.

Grubbs drove and sipped coffee as though he hardly needed to see the road. He seemed to know the way, so I saw no point in guiding him over the route I'd driven on Sunday.

Grubbs rang the doorbell, and we waited a minute. I leaned around and rang the bell a second time.

Paul Kramer answered the door, looking sleepy, his eyes swollen and unfocused. Grubbs offered him a business card. The kid took it and studied as though it were covered in hieroglyphics.

"I'm Captain Grubbs, Birmingham police department. This is Slate," Grubbs said. "We know this is not a good time, but we need to speak with Mrs. Kramer. Is she available?"

The boy looked up from the card at Grubbs, then peered under his hair at me.

"I'll see," he said, and shut the door in Grubbs' face.

I had to give the kid credit. Not many fifteen-year-olds would have closed the door on a police captain, even in mufti. But the family had been through a rough time, and he was, after all, Kramer's kid.

Thirty seconds later, the door was opened again by Susan Kramer. Today she wore a soft gray pants suit. She wore her hair up and pinned in back, and she appeared to have applied very little makeup. Aside from the gold crucifix, still in its place on a heavy gold chain, the only jewelry she wore was a wedding ring. Her eyes were red-rimmed, but that was the only outward sign of grief.

"Captain Grubbs."

Grubbs took the proffered hand for a moment and gave her a tiny nod that managed to convey sympathy and respect.

"I am Susan Kramer. I apologize for Paul. We've had a difficult night here. I suppose we should talk. But the police sergeant and lieutenant were here for several hours. I really don't know what else I can say."

Grubbs nodded. "This is Slate," he said.

"Mr. Slate," she said, extending her hand. She looked at Grubbs. "We have met."

We shook. Her hand was warm and dry.

"That's all right, Mrs. Kramer," I said. "I understand. We wanted to speak with you if you had a minute. Just a few questions."

I gestured toward the threshold. "May I?" I asked.

She stepped aside, and I walked into the foyer and took off my coat. The boy, Paul, was lurking in the entrance to the living room.

"Paul, take Mr. Slate's coat," said Mrs. Kramer.

The boy took my coat without a word and without meeting my eyes and hung it on a coat rack in the foyer.

Grubbs kept his jacket on, and we both followed Kramer's widow through the foyer toward a living room on the right.

Grubbs stopped me at the entrance to the living room.

"Slate, I need to speak with Mrs. Kramer first," he said. "Alone."

I had expected Grubbs to insist on a solo interview. "I'll wait," I said.

"Mr. Slate, why don't you sit in the library while I speak with the captain? It's just across the foyer." Susan Kramer pointed to the room to the left of the foyer, where Kramer had introduced me to the two FBI agents, with its floor-to-ceiling books, red silk upholstery, and writing table under the window.

I nodded. Grubbs followed the widow into the living room and closed the door behind him.

Unfilled with people, the library in the Kramer home looked comfortable. Warm. Used. I sat in the big armchair in the corner between the front window and the bookshelves, where Paul Kramer had been sitting while the two FBI agents interviewed him. One of the shelves across the room was devoted to family photographs: Don and Susan Kramer and the kids on a beach; a larger framed copy of the picture of Kris that Kramer had given me in my office.

I studied the room for clues to Kris's disappearance or Kramer's murder, but as far as I could tell there were none, so I took out my iPhone and pretended to be checking my email.

Susan Kramer sat composed and straight-backed across her living room from me. Grubbs had spent a little over ten minutes with her before he came out to take my place in the library. Only the right thumb and index finger fidgeting with the ring on her left hand betrayed any emotion. She smiled a little, but only with her mouth.

"Tell me again about how Don came to hire you?" she said.

I told her about Kramer's visit on Saturday.

She nodded a little, tentative, vague. "Don didn't always tell me every detail of his schedule. But he told me he was going to speak with someone else. Someone who had been recommended to him by someone he knew."

I told her I had known her husband years earlier when he worked in Montgomery.

She shook her head. "I know I sounded foolish the other day, maybe even belligerent. I should not have treated you in that manner. After all, 'What use is it for a man to say he has faith when he does nothing to show it?' Don told me later you were a person he'd been told had – helped – several people with – missing children. It's just that I thought I should have been consulted."

"Well. Helping people with interesting problems – including missing children – is something I've done, a little, in the last few years. And no, you don't sound foolish, Mrs. Kramer. You sound like a woman who. . . ."

Tears began to well in Susan Kramer's eyes before I finished a sentence I wished I hadn't begun.

"I'm sorry, I. . . ."

She shook her head and dabbed at her eyes with a tissue. "I'm just trying to hold together right now, and I'm not sure I can handle this discussion and talk to the police on the same day. Maybe if we talked a little later?"

"I understand. I'll check in with you tomorrow. In the meantime I'll make some inquiries on my own."

"Is that really necessary? I mean, with the FBI already looking, and now the police investigating, and so long as my faith is strong, it seems to me that, I don't know, is this really necessary?"

"I don't blame you for asking. Don seemed to think so, and sometimes it helps to have someone outside law enforcement in these matters."

Mrs. Kramer stood. "Thank you, Mr. Slate. I'm sure Don had his reasons. We appreciate your help."

"Just one more thing before I go."

"What is it?"

"I'd like to see Kris's room."

Susan Kramer shrugged, a gesture that seemed to fortify her. "All right. I'll show you. Right this way."

She led me to the stairway in the foyer. "Kris's room is to the left at the top of the stairs, straight down at the end of the hall. The door is closed, and the FBI agents already looked through it, but go on in. I don't know if it will help. She was only here on visits, really, since she moved to the campus."

I waited. "Oh. I'm not going up with you. I don't like to go in there since she . . . since she went missing. Was there something else?"

"Yes. Your husband and I didn't talk about any facts. I know only that Kris is missing. I know it's difficult, but could you tell me how you learned. . . .?"

"Kris's roommate, or suitemate, at school. She called my husband at his office in the morning. Said that Kris told her she was going to the library to study the night before. Her suitemate said she stayed up reading and then went to sleep. When she woke up the next morning, Kris wasn't there and her bed hadn't been slept in. She tried her cell phone and didn't get an answer. That's not like Kris. She was an athlete. She wasn't into parties or anything. She treasured her sleep. Always, since she was little. . . ."

"Thank you, Mrs. Kramer. What is Kris's roommate's name?"

"Akilah. Akilah Ziyenge. One of her soccer teammates."

"Okay. I'll just go up and look at the room now. I can let myself out."

The door to the room was closed. I opened it, went in, and closed the door softly behind me.

The air inside was still, the room silent. It was the room of a typical teenage girl post-Title IX, a girl consumed with active sports, not music or drugs or boys.

A sleigh bed, framed by windows, stood in the center of an outside wall. A net bag half-filled with scuffed soccer balls occupied one corner.

Cream walls almost completely covered with posters of soccer stars in action. In one, Mia Hamm raised her arms in triumph, a huge smile splitting her face. Another poster featured a grimacing Hope Solo crouching to prepare for a penalty kick.

And one small poster almost hidden by posters of recent or active players featured an ageless Pelé, body parallel to the ground in a bicycle kick, the great thigh muscles looking as inhuman as oiled machinery.

I didn't search any drawers or look under the bed for clues. The Birmingham police, detective novels to the contrary, would have been as thorough as the KGB. After absorbing the visual patterns, I stood at the foot of the bed, closed my eyes and entered into the stillness of the closed room, the only movement my breath. My inhalations and exhalations connected us; I was the room, the room was me.

What do you have to tell me, Kris? Are you out there somewhere? What are your secrets? Why have I heard different versions of when you were last seen? Do you want to be found?

After a couple of minutes, I didn't have any more answers than I'd ever had, so I opened the door, closed it softly behind me, walked down the stairs and let myself out of the house.

Grubbs was waiting in his car with the engine running. When I got in, he drove away without a word.

CHAPTER EIGHT

The board of trustees of Alabama Southern probably started every meeting with a prayer that God would move the campus to another location.

If they didn't, they should.

Alabama Southern squatted just off I-20 near the rotting old stadium called Legion Field, in a neighborhood otherwise filled with crack houses, shot houses, shooting galleries, boom boxes and nightly gunfire.

Businesses move. Upwardly mobile couples build, buy, sell, trade, swap houses like old men at a coin show.

But once a college decides on a campus location, it's pretty much stuck there. During real-estate bubbles or during the recessions that follow, there isn't much of a market for a nice, clean-but-lived-in early-70's biology building.

So Alabama Southern opted for the only alternative: they got serious about security long before September 11, 2001. They surrounded the campus with a twelve-foot fence of brick pillars and wrought-iron spikes. They installed gates with twenty-four-hour guards and security cameras.

To a visitor from out of town, these measures probably seemed paranoid or elitist. To Birmingham natives, they were no more than a display of common sense.

I had an appointment with the chief of the campus police at two o'clock in the afternoon. After Grubbs dropped me at the hotel, I had a sandwich sent up to my room, read through the notes in the *qui tam* file again, then took off my shoes, lay down on the bed, and rested for twenty minutes. Then I washed and dried my face, put my shoes and coat back on, collected my rental car, and took the ramp to I-59/I-20 South.

The Alabama Southern campus sat just east of the interstate off the Arkadelphia Road exit. I had a note from Leon Grubbs to show to the campus cop manning the gate a hundred yards inside the road approaching the campus. The cop nodded when he saw my note and told me to wait. He stepped inside his little guard house and spoke into his radio. Then he raised the red and white stick gate and gave me a half-wave, half salute.

The administration building could have housed the HQ at a Marine base: three stories, rambling, an indeterminate beige concrete on the exterior.

Inside, the building had a peculiar odor; not unpleasant, a mix of county courthouse and floral shop. An office directory on the wall near the elevators directed campus police department visitors to the basement.

I took the stairs.

Square green plastic signs suspended from the ceiling pointed to the right above the legend: Director of Campus Security. The chief's office suite occupied the northwestern corner of the basement.

An efficient-looking woman wearing a dark blue police uniform, who could have been any age from late twenties to fifty, sat at a computer desk. She had short dark brown hair and unpolished fingernails. She was busy at a keyboard but paused when I walked in.

"You must be Mr. Slate," she said.

"It's just Slate. I have an appointment with the chief."

She nodded without smiling. "The director is expecting you. It will be just a moment. Take a seat if you wish." She turned back to the keyboard.

On the wall facing her desk were framed photographs of a man in a police uniform with persons of note who had presumably visited the campus at some time: George H. W. Bush, Eddie Murphy, Hillary Clinton, William F. Buckley, Jr.

The odds of my appearing on the chief's wall seemed slim.

"Mr. Slate?"

"Just Slate."

"Oh, yes. Slate. Well, the director is ready for you. You may go on in."

Chief John Miller looked too young for a Southern police chief, even of a college police department. The face was unlined, and the nearly-black hair looked as though he spent too much to maintain it.

Miller wore a dark gray business suit with a white button-down shirt. The coat hung on a wooden coat rack in the corner behind the door. His tie had red and white stars sprinkled on a blue background. I felt more comfortable already.

We shook hands, and Miller sat behind a large desk with lots of overhang. I sat across from him in a dark red leather chair. More photos of Miller with celebrities hung on the wall behind the desk. I didn't see any family pictures.

Miller got right to the point. "I understand that Don Kramer hired you to investigate the disappearance of his daughter."

"Your understanding is correct."

Miller shrugged. "I've always tried to know something about the people who come to see me. Especially if they're coming to investigate a missing student. Kris Kramer's disappearance takes on a little more meaning for all of us now that her father appears to have been murdered."

I shrugged. "For some maybe. Any young woman's unexplained disappearance merits immediate investigation. Miss Kramer became important to me when her father hired me."

"Understood." Expressionless, Miller nodded.

"How long have you been Director of Campus Security?"

One corner of Miller's mouth turned up, just a little.

"They gave me that title in January of 2002. I've been chief of the campus police here for almost fifteen years."

"Lots of policemen became directors of security after September 2001."

"Lots of new titles, a little more money. Nothing else different."

"You have a lot of missing students here at Southern?"

Miller shook his head. "Three in my time here. One turned up in New Orleans with her boyfriend. Another turned out to be a Jane Doe admitted to the psych ward at the charity hospital in Atlanta."

"And then Kris."

"Then Kris. I was counting Kris in the three, but the other two were last seen on this campus. Officially, Kris Kramer is not missing from campus. She was last seen somewhere else."

"Where?"

Miller's eyes widened a hair. "I would have thought you already knew that."

I shrugged. "You don't know, you ask a question."

Miller nodded. "My department's investigation showed that Kris was last seen by her mother when they were both leaving Park Plaza downtown."

"Her father's law office."

Miller opened an ivory folder on his desk and scanned it.

"Correct. Afternoon of Thursday January 19. Mother and daughter had been to see the father at his law firm. My notes say the mother drove to Indian Hills Academy to pick up Kris's little brother. Kris has not been seen on campus since."

Susan Kramer had told me Kris's suitemate saw Kris the evening before she disappeared, not that she was the last person to see Kris. Mrs. Kramer had also said that the suitemate had called Kramer's law office when Kris did not answer her cell phone. Don Kramer had believed that Susan Kramer was the last person to see Kris before her disappearance. "Did your people interview anyone here on campus?"

"Sure. Roommate, soccer coach, professors. Not much there. She didn't show up for any classes and appears not to have spoken with anyone here after she left the campus on Thursday."

"Would you mind if I looked through your file?"

"No, but I can do better than that."

He turned to a keyboard at his left and typed a few strokes. The office door opened, and Miller's secretary walked in and took the folder.

"We're on the same team. Celeste will make a complete copy for you. Anything else you need, let me know."

"There is something I need. I need to interview Kris's roommate."

Miller gestured toward the monitor. "Transcript of our interview with the roommate is in the file. I probably shouldn't even be giving you that, but, hey, maybe you see something we didn't, it helps locate the girl. But as to an interview, I have to say no. No interviews with the roommate. No interviews with any students."

"Sounds pretty cut and dried, Chief."

"It's the law, Slate. You're a lawyer. Buckley Amendment. Kid breaks his leg at a frat football game, we need a release to call his mother."

Miller stood. "The file you're getting will give you some information that might help you look for Kris Kramer. But you will not find any other student's name. This school will not get sued on my account."

I stood and shook Miller's hand. "Just one thing. Since we're on the same team, I assume your people won't mind if I hang around campus and talk to the few people here who aren't students. Am I right?"

"You're welcome here on my – on the campus, but I don't think you'll learn much. Kris wasn't here when she disappeared."

"More than I knew yesterday, Chief."

Celeste had a copy of the material from the department's file in another ivory folder for me as soon as I stepped outside Miller's office. Efficient. Or in a hurry to get rid of me. One thing I knew. Miller was damn sure – and damn glad – the girl hadn't disappeared from campus.

The athletic complex was on the back side of the campus, down the hill toward the interstate.

A thick copse of woods separated the campus from the highway, and the soccer stadium where both the Alabama Southern men and women played NAIA soccer games was the last clear space before the woods. The Physical Education department and athletic offices occupied a low three-story beige structure that hugged the hill above the stadium.

There was no receptionist or security desk on the ground floor. A black locator board with white letters indicated that the soccer offices were on the second floor. A sweeping cast iron circular stairway in the center of the building led to the second and third floors.

The second floor corridor walls were filled with photos of former soccer players, framed media guide covers, framed photos of teams from each year of the program with won-loss records and statistics.

Kris Kramer was a freshman. No team picture for this year. No team picture might ever include Kris Kramer.

I continued down the hall until I reached the end of the corridor. The men's soccer head coach's office was on the left, the women's on the right. Both had doors of pebbled glass with the coaches' names etched inside an opaque strip at eye level.

The name of the women's coach was Sarah Kronenberg.

There were no lights on the men's side. A narrow band of light striped the carpet at the bottom of the women's coach's office, however, and light filtered weakly through the translucent glass into the corridor.

I pushed on the door. It opened onto a small office with a couple of inexpensive waiting-room chairs and a desk.

The room was empty. To the right of the desk was a solid wooden door. I crossed to the door. I could hear faint sounds inside. I knocked twice and opened the door.

Inside, a woman with a blonde pixie haircut was sitting on the dark blue carpet with her back against a sofa covered in burgundy vinyl. She wore gray sweatpants and a black long-sleeved tee shirt. Her feet were bare.

A flat-panel television monitor hung on the opposite wall. A couple of remotes lay on the floor beside the woman. In front of her on the carpet was a notebook computer. Aside from the light from the monitors, the room was dark.

The woman clicked the remote and scrambled to her feet when she saw me. She brushed off her hand and stuck it out.

"Hello," she said. "Sally Kronenberg. I wasn't expecting anyone around. I was just watching film of last season. We'll be starting spring soccer in a few weeks."

I shook the coach's hand. The handshake was firm and dry, the fingers a little blocky for a woman, the nails short and unpolished. She did not appear to be wearing makeup. The red streaks in her eyes could have resulted from recent tears or from too much time in front of screens in a darkened room.

"Slate. I hate to interrupt your work, Coach, but it's important that we talk. I'm trying to find Kris Kramer."

Sally Kronenberg nodded a little. "We'd all like to find Kris. I know her parents are – were – Ohh."

Her chest heaved slightly and she bit her lip. "Well, I understand the FBI is doing everything it can. Don't take this the wrong way, but – uhh – they didn't mention you. Are you with the police, or something?"

"No. Private. Don Kramer came to see me on Saturday and hired me to find his missing daughter. So far I haven't accomplished very much, and I really need to talk with you. Have you spoken with the police?"

"Yes, it was a Captain, uh, African-American fellow."

"Leon Grubbs."

"Captain Grubbs. Yeah, that's right. He didn't tell me his first name. Neither did you."

"Slate is enough. Here."

I took out one of Grubbs' cards and gave it to her. "Call Grubbs, uh, Captain Grubbs. I think he'll vouch for me."

She took the card and studied it for a second, then looked up at me and nodded. "Would you mind waiting outside for just a moment?"

"No, I don't mind." I walked out into the exterior office and heard the bolt turn after the door closed.

Two minutes later the door opened, and Coach Kronenberg motioned me in.

"All right," she said. "You are who you say you are. I'll be glad to do whatever I can to help find Kris. All the young women who play soccer for me are like family."

"Why did you lock me out of the office while you called?"

The coach smiled a little. "My father was a police officer in Chicago for twenty-five years. I can spot a concealed pistol from half a block. And I didn't want you to hear me call Captain Grubbs, either. I can be pretty blunt."

"No need to apologize."

"I wasn't apologizing." A small lift of the eyebrows. A challenge? "So you're looking for Kris Kramer," she said. "What did Don Kramer tell you?"

That was an interesting question. I was, however technically, still a member of the Alabama bar. Under United States law, attorney-client privilege does not die with the client.

During the Whitewater investigation, the Office of the Independent Counsel tried to obtain copies of the files of James Hamilton, Esq., the lawyer who had represented Vincent W. Foster, Jr. Foster was Deputy White House Counsel, a close confidant of President William Jefferson Clinton and his wife, later Senator and Secretary of State, Hilary Rodham Clinton – some said especially of the wife – and he had been found shot dead on the mall near the Washington Monument.

Independent Counsel Kenneth Starr was, therefore, somewhat interested in Vincent Foster.

Foster's lawyer objected to the subpoena.

Considering that objection, the United States Court of Appeals for the District of Columbia Circuit held that the attorney-client privilege "weakens" after the client's death, and ordered Hamilton to turn over his files.

Hamilton appealed the issue to the United States Supreme Court. The Supreme Court reversed the lower court and held, 6-3, that "[i]t has been generally . . . accepted, for well over a century, that the attorney-client privilege survives the death of the client in a case such as this."

The fact that a lawyer was consulted, however, is not privileged, even while the client is alive, and I had already told the coach that I'd been hired to find Kris Kramer.

"Don Kramer traveled to my office in Gulf Shores on Saturday and hired me to look for Kris. I'm a lawyer, but looking for missing persons is – uhh – something I do." I didn't see any point in telling her my office was in the back of a bar.

Kronenberg walked back to the desk at the end of the room underneath the window and stuck her feet into a pair of blue thongs. Then she opened a desk drawer and clipped on a small black leather fanny pack.

"Let's not talk here. I'm seeing soccer balls in my sleep, these days. Would you like to get a cup of coffee?"

"All right," I said. "I'll follow you, Coach."

On the second floor of the student union building, the coffee shop commanded a view of the dormitory quadrangle through huge double-hung windows. For some reason the shop was named The Basement.

I ordered a medium regular coffee. The coach ordered a tall skinny latté, and we settled in at a small table beneath one of the windows.

Coach Kronenberg poured a blue packet of Equal into her latté, stirred, then looked up at me. "Well, Mr. Slate. I don't know what you know and what you don't know," she said. "So why don't you start?"

"I don't know much." I told her about Kramer's visit to Gulf Shores and about the early morning phone call from Grubbs and identifying Kramer's body. I left out the part about the rain falling into his unseeing eyes.

Sally Kronenberg didn't say a word while I spoke. Her eyes stayed locked on mine.

When I finished, she picked up her latté and took a sip. "Coffee here is good," she said. "'One hundred per cent Columbian,' like the sign says."

"Yeah. Not bad. I read somewhere it's the roast, though, not the beans."

"I wouldn't know. I just drink the stuff. So. What do you want to know?"

"What kind of girl is Kris Kramer?"

"You're hoping I will tell you I suspect she does drugs or is into kinky sex or something."

"I just need to know the facts."

She cocked her head to one side. "Just the facts, ma'am."

"Something like that."

She shook her head enough to make the hair on the sides of her face swing past her cheeks. "If a missing girl was into drugs or bad boys, it would make it easier to start looking for her, wouldn't it?"

"I suppose so. There would be a place to start, the end of the thread to start pulling."

She was silent for a moment, sipping her coffee, a slightly faraway look in her eyes. "I'm sorry," she said. "Kris is one of the best girls I've ever coached. Incredible work ethic. Smart. Steady. No drugs. No bad boys. No boys at all as far as I know."

"No boys?"

"No girls either." She took another small sip of her latte. A tiny bit of foam clung to her lower lip. "Not all female athletes are lesbians, Mr. Slate."

I had a sip of my own coffee, now almost cool enough to drink. "I may be a redneck," I said. "But even I know that."

"Umm." She made a little motion with her head that could have been agreement or affirmation or a neurological twitch.

"Did Kris seem particularly religious?"

She shook her head slowly. "No, I wouldn't say so. We have an FCA — Fellowship of Christian Athletes — Chapter here, and some of my girls participate, but I don't recall that Kris did. Of course, we are a church-affiliated school, so perhaps more of the athletes here are observant than, say, would be the case at a state university."

"Which church?"

"Episcopal."

"Not Catholic?"

"No. I suppose you've met Kris's mother. I understand that she is quite devout. But Kris didn't seem to be. More like her father, I guess."

We sat without speaking. Through the big old windows of the student union building, I could see students moving about the campus with a purpose. To ward off the damp and chill of the Alabama winter, many wore technical outer gear that would have sufficed for a Himalayan expedition.

Into the silence, the coach said, "I think you should talk with Kris's roommate."

"So do I. The chief – excuse me, the director of campus security – didn't think it was necessary, though."

"I wouldn't want to get into any trouble with the police, Mr. Slate. But if you were back in my office in, say, thirty minutes, and Kris's roommate just happened to be there too, I couldn't stop you from talking, could I?"

She smiled, stood, and stretched. "This cold weather makes me want to be in front of a fire on a blanket. See you around, Slate."

Akilah Ziyenge was just under six feet tall. Her hair was in braids, and she spoke with a British accent. We talked in the assistant women's soccer coach's office.

"How long were you and Kris roommates?" I asked her.

"Just this year. Kris was a freshman. I'm a junior. Coach K likes to have the younger girls room with the older players. And we're both goalkeepers."

"You're both tall."

She smiled. "Yeah. Right position for us."

"Do you know Kris well?"

"We share a suite – separate bedrooms. But I consider us roommates. I know her pretty well."

"Where did you last see her?"

"In the suite. She came earlier that day to pick up some things. She was with her mother, and I thought she was going home for the weekend."

"What day was that?"

"Thursday."

"Okay. Was that unusual? For Kris to come by with her mother?"

"I don't know. I'd seen her mother here before, but it wasn't common. Not sure her mother had ever just come by to pick her up. I saw her Dad more often. He's a soccer fan, you know, really into sports. He was always hanging around. Sometimes came by to watch practice."

"Did Kris get along well with her mother?"

Akilah nodded slowly. "As far as I know. I mean, I don't know of any big arguments they had or anything. Yeah, they weren't much alike in a way, but they got along."

"But then Kris came back that night?"

"After she left with her mother? No. Like I said, she took books and her laptop and some clothes like she was going home for the weekend."

"Do you remember anything special Kris said or did while she was there? Anything she and her mother were talking about?"

"No. Nothing they said." She shook her head. "No."

"Something else?"

"Not really."

"All right. Was Kris seeing anybody special, any guys or anything, that you knew about?"

"No, not Kris. She told me her Dad wanted her to concentrate on school and soccer this first year. She really tried to put her head down and work hard. She said her Dad told her if she didn't do that at least this year, she'd never know what she could do.

"I mean, it's not like, she's not a toad, though, you know? We hang around a little with some of the guys on the men's team, but nothing serious like that was going on."

"And you'd know, right?"

"Right." Akilah nodded a few more times than necessary, as though she'd made up her mind about something. "You said was there anything else that day."

"Yes."

"There was. I don't know why and I don't know what it means, but she gave me something to hold for her."

Her backpack was on the floor beside her chair. She unzipped one of the outside compartments, pulled out a small object and held it out to me.

I held out my palm, and she placed it there. Her fingers were long and strong, the nails short but red-lacquered. The object was a USB keychain memory device. "Do you know what's on it?"

"No clue. But. . . ."

"What?"

"Kris told me when she gave me the memory stick that she wanted me to keep it safe and that she'd trust me to know if I needed to let someone else see it." She smiled a little, one corner of her mouth going up, blinking back a tear.

"Did Kris mention the memory stick to you earlier, when her mother was there?"

She thought a minute, then shook her head. "No."

She brushed a hand across her eyes. "Mr. Slate, do you think anything bad has happened to Kris? I wasn't too worried at first, but now I'm starting to feel really bad. Her dad getting shot . . . Do you think whatever is on the memory stick has anything to do with Kris disappearing? Or with her Dad?"

My gut told me yes. "Did you look at it?"

She shook her head. "I tried after Kris didn't come back on Sunday night or Monday. But I couldn't open anything. It looked like the files might be encrypted."

I told her she'd done the right thing.

"Yeah," she said. "I think so too. Coach K likes you, and, you know, Coach K knows about police and stuff." She stood up. "Well, I've got a lab. Bye, now." And just like that, she was out the door and gone.

When I went to look for Coach Kronenberg, her office door was locked, and the building suddenly seemed very empty.

I let myself out.

CHAPTER NINE

Wednesday January 25

I hadn't brought funeral clothing to Birmingham. The blue blazer and gray slacks I'd worn the day before were the best I could do, along with the white shirt I'd sent to the hotel laundry.

Light rain had returned for Kramer's funeral. My clothing didn't matter. It was a season for raincoats.

I had been to only one other burial service at Elmwood Cemetery, for one of Anna's aunts on her mother's side. I asked for directions from the hotel concierge because I wanted to be there early and watch the other mourners arrive.

The rain had slowed to a drizzle by the time I found the main gates, but the cemetery's oaks still dripped water.

Don Kramer was buried within sight of the final resting place of Paul "Bear" Bryant and within earshot of the grave of the black jazz musician Sun Ra. Death treats all of us as equals, even in Birmingham, Alabama.

Graveside workers from the funeral home and the cemetery were at the gravesite before I arrived. I stood a discreet distance away, hands folded in front.

Soon automobiles began easing through the gates. Directed by cemetery officials, they rolled to the side of one of the cemetery paths, part of the labyrinth that wound through the acres of burial grounds, and stopped, their engines tick-ticking in the cold damp air.

Members of the bar, the judiciary, government officials, businessmen filed past me, some nodding. I remained at the edge of the crowd, not far from some of the parked cars, but I spotted a former Birmingham mayor and two former governors.

At precisely ten o'clock, the black hearse drew up, followed by a couple of limousines and the private automobiles of family members.

Six of Kramer's law partners served as pallbearers; I recognized Bill Woolf, a head taller than most of the men.

The funeral director efficiently seated the family, and the service began. From my position on a slight rise a little apart from the crowd, the mourners' backs, a mass of dark suits, raincoats, a few umbrellas, seemed to absorb the weak daylight.

A former president of the American Bar Association, the silver-haired named partner of a big downtown Birmingham firm, gave the eulogy. From what I could hear, he told the mourners that he and Kramer had been enemies in the courtroom but comrades at the bar.

Bill Woolf spoke briefly, most of his words, directed, it seemed, to the family, and inaudible to me.

Kramer's priest read the burial service and closed with a prayer. A cemetery worker touched a switch on the chrome-plated frame holding the bronze casket, and it began descending smoothly into the grave.

Some of the mourners near me began drifting toward their cars. Close family sat, still as statues, in the portable chairs set up by the funeral home.

A breeze flapped the cornices of the burial tent. The priest stood over Susan Kramer, offering soft words to her and the family. At last, he nodded and moved to the other side of the tent to speak to some of the people from the law firm who had lingered.

The family members stood. The funeral director spoke to Susan Kramer, taking her hand in both of his.

Some of the workers rolled away the green carpet, uncovered a pile of earth. Shovels appeared, and they began to fill in the grave.

Paul Kramer suddenly moved away from his mother and toward one of the workers. He said a word or two to the man, who nodded slowly and stepped back.

The man's shovel was now in the boy's hand. Paul Kramer filled and emptied the shovel with an economy of movement I would not have expected, lightly tossing the earth into his father's grave. Although I was too far away to see clearly, his face appeared wet in the uncertain light.

"Slate?" Leon Grubbs stood a pace away on my right. I had not seen him earlier.

"Captain."

"Sad funeral," Grubbs said.

"I've never seen a happy one. Pretty soon after the death, don't you think?"

"Maybe. I got the coroner's office moving. Autopsy occurred early in the morning after the family was notified. Wake was last night. Mass early this morning. Next day burial. Part of the culture in the Jewish and Islamic traditions, though not necessarily the Catholic." He shrugged. "Anyway, I think you know more about all this than you've told me so far."

"Maybe I know less than you think."

"Right. Since it's you, that possibility occurred to me as well." He shook his head. "If you know anything, you need to share it. Understood?"

I nodded. "I understand."

Grubbs turned and started walking toward his car, then turned back to face me. "Slate," he said.

"Yeah?" I traced his steps, and we stood two feet apart.

"I'm going to give you some free information so you don't waste your time," Grubbs said. "Kramer had not arranged a meeting with any kidnappers, at least not to pay a ransom. We've reviewed all his bank and brokerage accounts. Nothing. No cash withdrawals, no wires, no unusual transactions at all."

"All right," I said. "Thanks. At least I don't have to ask Mrs. Kramer about that."

Grubbs nodded. "Another reason to tell you now. Besides, reporters are calling my office so often I had to put an administrative assistant on press duty full time. A morning press conference at which I have nothing to report has become a part of my day since the day after Kris Kramer was reported missing. Her father's death will increase the number of reporters in my briefing room exponentially. Some of these facts will be in my statement to the press pool tomorrow morning. You heard it here first.

"See you around, Slate."

It was almost noon. Don Kramer's burial service was over, the family getting into the limousines, the cars lined up in single file, exhausts making steam clouds in the cool damp air.

I needed to return to lower Alabama, to the boat and the bar for more clothes and to take down more systems for a longer absence.

I had time to get back to the hotel for lunch and to pick up the files Kramer gave me, then I had one more appointment on the Southside of Birmingham before I drove to the airport.

CHAPTER TEN

Smolian Psychiatric Clinic perched on Seventh Avenue South in the complex of buildings known locally as UAB, seventy-five city blocks on the south side of the railroad tracks that run northeast to southwest through Birmingham and bisect the city as the Thames bisects London.

America remembers Birmingham for Bull Connor and his fire hoses, "A Letter from the Birmingham Jail." But that was nearly fifty years ago. For two decades Birmingham's mayor has been African-American.

Old Birmingham called itself The Football Capital of the South. The stadium with that slogan painted on the bottom of the upper deck sits quietly rusting on the west side of I-65. In the new Birmingham, neither Auburn nor Alabama has played a football game for years.

Birmingham reinvented itself as the medical center and engineering capital of the South. The UAB Health Services Foundation built the "third-largest ambulatory clinic in the world," as I once heard it described at a cocktail party by the gushing wife of the financial VP of the foundation. I.M. Pei designed the building. It was called the Kirklin Clinic after the famous heart surgeon George Wallace lured there from the Mayo Clinic in the sixties.

The state built the clinic and created the foundation so the school could continue to attract famous M.D.'s who expect to make a million dollars a year, minimum. Alabama could never afford to allow Alabama citizens, forty per cent of whom did not graduate from high school, know that it was paying that kind of money to employees, even doctors.

So they set the clinic up as a private foundation, and the foundation paid most of the good doctors' salaries. Off the school's books, off the tax rolls, perfectly legal – and out of the public eye.

The Smolian building was not designed by I.M. Pei. Psychiatry doesn't attract the revenue stream to justify expensive clinical offices. Smolian's architecture was more 1950s-public-clinic than 1990s-famous-architect.

Dr. Beverly Adams' office was on the third floor. The geriatric elevator opened a dozen feet in front of a glass cubicle housing reception and billing.

The only other persons in the lobby were a small family, mother, father, and pre-school son, talking quietly in a corner.

Renee, the receptionist, greeted me with her usual smile that managed to convey warmth and professional distance simultaneously. "Good afternoon, Mr. Slate," she said. "Please sit down. Dr. Adams will be available in just a few minutes."

It was four minutes by the big clock above the reception window. It had never been more than eight. Punctuality was one advantage of consulting academic physicians. Their government salaries diminished the need to overbook private patients.

"You can go back now, Mr. Slate," Renee said with that schizophrenic smile.

My psychiatrist was waiting for me at the door of her office down a corridor along the outside of the building.

Bev Adams was forty-five, tall but not angular, with blonde hair worn at chin length and gray eyes. She had graduated second in her undergraduate class at Cornell and in the top ten at Harvard medical school.

She hadn't told me that herself, but I'd learned all I could about her before my first appointment.

The corridor was lined with windows; Dr. Adams' tiny office, just large enough for her desk and its chair, a filing cabinet, and a chair for her patients, was windowless. I followed her into the office, and we took our places.

"How are you?" she said.

Every session began this way. Here, in this building, in this relationship, unlike almost anywhere else on earth, the expected answer to that question was not necessarily "Fine."

In fact but implicitly, there was no expected answer to that question, here. There was no anticipation at all. This moment between that question and my answer was the moment in every session with Bev Adams that I anticipated most and from which I derived the most benefit, if not pleasure.

I had never told her that, and I probably never would.

Bev waited. I breathed once. In. Out. My breath like a gate. Swinging open. Swinging shut. "I've been better," I said.

"What do you want to tell me?"

A missing girl. Her father dead. And as always, my dreams.

Five years and seven months had gone by since the accident.

We'd been driving back from the beach on the first Sunday in June. Anna and David were in the Volvo just ahead of me.

I followed, alone in the Toyota because I'd driven down earlier in the week for a conference, and Anna wanted David to ride with her. In the safer car.

It wasn't safe enough. The eighteen wheeler crossed the median, its driver asleep, swiped aside a Camaro and hit the Volvo head on.

No car is safe in that kind of accident. I stopped and got out and ran and looked – once. And thus began life alone.

After the funeral, I'd gone in to the law office every day for six months. But after I wound up Anna's estate and settled – too cheaply – with the trucking company, I wrote a cordial letter of resignation to my

senior partner at Steiner & Sayre, rented the house to a visiting professor of medicine from the University of Geneva, loaded the Toyota with
clothes and books, and drove south until there was no more land.

"They were taken away, Bev." I liked to say her name. Not long after,
long stretches of time floated away when I uttered no other woman's
name. "They aren't coming back."

"Those are the facts. But how do you feel?"

I wasn't sure. What was the right answer? Depressed? In pain? I
settled for the truth.

"Mostly sort of numb."

"Walling yourself off from your feelings will just prolong the heal-
ing process."

"You never sugar-coat your advice."

"I'm not Mary Poppins. You know that."

"And you're not Dear Abby, either."

"Our sessions are about your feelings, not about what I learned in
medical school."

Oh, yes. My feelings. Not the facts, just the feelings, sir. Well, most
of the time my feelings suck. "Living is all about suffering."

"But a way out of suffering exists. That's the third of the noble
truths, right?"

"Yes."

"Are you working?"

"A little. There isn't much to do with the bar right now. I do have
some – uhh – legal work."

"How does that feel to you?"

I wasn't sure. "My client hired me to find his missing daughter.
Then my client died."

"If you were like most of my patients, I would ask at this point if
you think you're depressed, and, perhaps, I would ask if you ever think
of suicide."

"But you won't ask me."

"Because we have established that you are not like my other patients."

"I don't know your other patients. But we have determined that I do not think of suicide."

"Do you still carry a gun?"

"Yes."

"For your work."

"For my work, on general principles."

When I applied for a carry permit at the Baldwin County sheriff's office and hesitated when I reached the space on the form that asked for the reason for the application, the clerk told me to write the word "protection" in the blank. It's a dangerous world. And a gun is a tool for coping with that world, a piece of fine machinery to be used, respected, cared for. Like a Swiss watch, a computer, an airplane.

"You are not suicidal now?"

"No."

"If I thought you were, I'd have to ask you to let me keep the gun."

"If I were suicidal, I'd let you keep it."

"Or maybe not." A slight frown, then a nod, as though she'd resolved something and filed it. "How is your libido?"

My libido. "Could we talk about suicide again?"

"Why? Is your libido suicidal?"

For whatever prehensile reason, I thought of Sally Kronenberg sitting cross-legged on her office floor. "Actually, no. I'm going to be okay, I think."

She smiled. "That's the goal."

CHAPTER ELEVEN

The lineman at the FBO used a diesel tow cart to move a Beechjet to clear a path out of the hangar for my Czech warbird. They'd washed the airplane, and it looked as though the tires had received a shot of air.

Ramp workers here and everywhere else this plane visited gave it a bit more care than they gave the Piper Warriors with bad paint.

I went inside the lobby of the FBO and checked the weather on the computer in the pilots' briefing room. Not so bad; high clouds but no more rain predicted for twenty-four hours. The air would be smooth. It was a good day for flying, and I needed to kick the tires and light the fires.

The little L-39 jet cruised at three hundred fifty knots, and it would do almost five hundred miles per hour at twenty thousand feet.

It also ate enough cash in maintenance and fuel every year to rent a nice house. In the Warsaw Pact countries, they'd called it the Albatros.

At Alabama I'd started to school on a football scholarship. Playing your high-school ball at a little north Alabama high school made standing out on film pretty easy; most of the other guys were scrappy but small, the rest fat and slow.

But it took only my freshman year for Coach Stallings' staff to see that with me they'd made a mistake, and by the end of the year I agreed. What I lacked in speed, size, and strength, I made up for through lack of discipline in the weight room.

Leaving the team was a mutual decision with no hard feelings.

By the time I was twenty, an electrical engineering major, I was paying my way to school working as a flight instructor. I'd earned my license and ratings swapping work for lessons, starting when I was fourteen, at a little country airport.

After college graduation I took a job with a commuter airline. On my days off, I flew as standby first officer on a Canadair business jet owned by one of the largest independent paper companies in the country.

After a year flying right seat in a Fairchild Metroliner and another two as captain, I was ready for law school.

The Metroliner was a decent airplane but noisy. Sitting in the flight cabin just in front of the tips of twin four-bladed propellers moving at supersonic speed, the captain and first officer wore earplugs and noise-attenuating headsets. Still, you would yell to hear yourself for an hour after a long flight.

But in law school, I discovered I still needed to fly. I joined the Air National Guard, did a couple of summers of basic, and ended up with a ride in a Phantom older than I was.

That's when I learned the definition of loud engines. Loud is an F-4 Phantom. From the pilot's chair, even with a helmet and earplugs, a Phantom at takeoff power sounds like all the beasts of hell in full wail at your back.

I spent two years flying the RF-4C Phantom on weekends and summer duty with the 117th Air National Guard Tactical Reconnaissance unit in Birmingham. Then in 1990 we got our Gulf War call-up.

My RIO and I flew low-level photo recon missions over Iraq nearly every day for three months until someone in Washington – no, probably Langley – thought Saddam had learned his lesson.

When I left Birmingham, I quit the Air Guard and didn't fly for three years.

But I kept my medical current. Late one afternoon in early September, I was sitting on a lawn chair on the beach in front of the Lost Lagoon looking idly at the last of the summer bikinis, and I looked up to watch a yellow Piper Super Cub in slow flight, trolling a banner advertising a new white tablecloth restaurant out on the old Fort Morgan Road.

I had probably seen the same airplane a hundred times, but that day, watching the little plane crawl across the azure sky, I experienced a feeling of loss I could explain only to another pilot, and the next morning I was in the shack which served as the office of the airport FBO asking if they had a flight instructor who could check me out in a rental plane.

Thirty minutes later I was at the controls of an aging Cessna 172 with lots of bare aluminum showing through the paint.

As we turned west, we could see down the Fort Morgan peninsula to Mobile Bay, south to Dauphin Island, and north to the intracoastal waterway that cuts off Gulf Shores and Orange Beach from the mainland of Baldwin County.

"Beautiful, id'n it?" the instructor shouted. I glanced at him and realized he was reacting to the huge grin on my face.

We flew west while the instructor yelled information in my ear about avoiding the Bon Secour national wilderness area and the importance of getting updated wind information before landing because of the shifting coastal breeze. Mostly I ignored him.

Back at the airport, I lined up on the same runway we'd taken off from, but now the wind was blowing about twelve or fifteen knots directly abeam the airplane as the Lycoming sputtered down final.

I cranked the right wing down against the breeze and held left rudder to hold the nose straight with a touch of extra airspeed for the gusts and only ten degrees of flaps instead of the usual thirty. The instructor sat stone-faced, his hands folded in his lap.

The plane touched down on its right main first. In a couple of hundred feet, the left main tire squeaked onto the asphalt as I continued to hold left rudder and right aileron. Finally, the nose tire kissed the pavement.

As we taxied back to the ramp, the instructor leaned over. "I told you you have to check the wind every time out here. But I'll say one thing. You're a helluva pilot."

I began to teach a few students again and to fly couples up and down the beach once in a while for an occasional sightseeing flight.

Then one morning after I'd checked on things at the bar and driven out to the airport to meet a student, I heard the high-pitched whine of a jet engine from a couple of miles away.

I figured maybe a member of the Blue Angels squadron in an FA-18 from over at Pensacola was doing some solo practice, but a few seconds later there was a small jet in camouflage paint entering the pattern for runway 6.

The airplane taxied to the ramp and shut down, and a balding guy in green coveralls took off a David Clark headset and climbed out of the cockpit.

After a brief conversation with the pilot, I was on the phone with Major Viktor Bedrosian of Cold War Jets in Talladega, Alabama.

After the Berlin Wall fell, after the breakup of the U.S.S.R., the former Soviet-bloc countries, particularly East Germany, Poland and Czechoslovakia, were long on military equipment and short on cash.

The Eastern bloc sold dozens of military surplus jet trainers, most of them practically new, along with spare parts – engines, wings, ejection seats, you name it – to nearly anyone with money in hand.

Cold War Jets bought out the entire East German Air Force supply of new L-39 parts, including forty-something engines. The jets were shipped in crates to Talladega and reassembled there with no changes aside from installation of U.S.-compatible radio and navigation equipment.

Major Bedrosian had retired from the former Soviet Air Force and now served as flight instructor.

I drove up to Talladega on a warm spring day. L-39s were not the only Soviet-bloc jet aircraft available there, and Major Bedrosian and I walked up and down the flight line looking at Iskras and L-29 Delfins as well as three assembled and ready-for-sale L-39s. The Iskras and L-29s were temptingly inexpensive, the price of a used single-engine Cessna. Major Bedrosian patiently explained the virtues and vices of all three models. Then he said, "You know what we used to say about the L-29? The only reason it ever lifts off is that the earth is curved." A three thousand foot takeoff roll is a seriously long takeoff roll for a jet, underpowered or not.

Like most Soviet-bloc-designed aircraft, the trainers were built to be dependable and rugged. The Pentagon must have war-gamed for every possible sort of conflict with the Soviets in Europe, and surely they were aware that Soviet aircraft were like the watches in the old Timex commercials – they could take a lickin' and keep on tickin'. So I wonder whether, if the conflict had stretched into weeks or months, the shorter supply lines and ruggedness of the Soviet weapons systems might not have made a decisive difference. Their military industries designed weapons to be used and reused in the field. The Mig-29, the Soviet bloc's air superiority fighter, had landing gear so rugged the airplane could operate from unimproved or bomb-damaged landing strips, and the engine inlets included grates that protected the engines from debris. In the U.S., more complex and fragile systems meant higher profits for the weapons industry, so – well. The world will never know.

Two of the L-39 aircraft for sale sported glowing new Imron paint and state-of-the-art glass cockpit avionics. A third aircraft, with low total time and a low-time engine, wore its original, slightly-faded Czech camouflage livery. The white paint on the landing gear was peeling in a couple of spots, and the avionics, though Westernized, displayed traditional steam gauges. This aircraft reminded me of the sometimes-ratty F-4s I had flown. The asking price was also a hundred thousand dollars lower than the prices of the shiny ones. I took a demonstration flight and signed the papers to acquire the airplane that afternoon.

The planes could be ordered with or without armed ejection seats. I chose the disarmed variety. In a plane that touches down dead-stick at ninety-five knots, firing the nineteen-sixties-era ejection seat is probably quite a bit riskier than an engine-out forced landing.

Outside, the lineman hooked a tow cart to the Albatros and deftly placed it in a space on the ramp.

When an airplane has sat in a strange shop for several days, a thorough preflight inspection is never a bad idea.

One of the instructors at Cold War Jets once took off in an Iskra that had just been pulled out of a hangar and lost the engine after climbing to three thousand feet. He was able to land on a road with no damage except to the engine. When the engine was torn down, inspectors found bits of painted aluminum metal inside the turbines.

Speculation was that someone had set an empty soft drink can inside the engine nacelle, and the preflight had overlooked it.

I drained and splashed fuel, opened the fuel caps to peer inside the fuel tanks, checked all the control surfaces, noted that the antennas were still in place.

When I finished looking over the airframe and engine for things that might kill me, I climbed inside and strapped myself into the seat. Engine start and takeoff were normal, and I climbed out and headed south on a perfect day for flying, quiet and still, high cirrus clouds and not much wind.

I remembered a flight in a National Guard F-4 on a training run flying I-R training routes over Mississippi and Arkansas, returning to Alabama late one afternoon, flying away from the setting sun and toward the rotation of the earth, when the air was smooth as butter and the aircraft seemed suspended in the velvety humid Mississippi air, while the Earth slipped slowly away beneath me.

Meditating, watching the breath, is like standing on a river bank and watching the water flow by. Flying, meditation, watching the river slip by, can sometimes reveal the real you underneath the monkey-mind busy-ness zinging around in your brain.

Jack Edwards Airport was in sight in a near-perfect half hour. I needed cases farther from home. Better if the clients stayed alive though.

The Toyota wouldn't start. The problem wasn't the flywheel this time, because the engine would spin, but no cylinders were firing. I trudged over to the fancy new FBO office where the corporate jet pilots hung out and asked to borrow the courtesy car.

The blonde at the desk reached behind her, and with inch-long red fingernails unhooked the keys to a Ford Escort. "Just fill it up," she said.

"No problem," I told her.

On the way to the marina, glancing to the right at the T-intersection of Alabama Highway 59 and Beach Boulevard, I could see my bar. Lost Lagoon. The sight felt like miles gone by. No time to stop in today.

A few weeks after I closed on the *Anna Grace*, the medical school professor had accepted a permanent position at the medical school in Birmingham and made an offer on the house. I made a counteroffer, and we reached a deal.

Two days after we'd closed, I'd walked into the Lost Lagoon Lounge and asked to see the owner. Another boat owner at the marina had told me he was moving back to New York and was looking for a buyer.

Six weeks later we met in a Gulf Shores lawyer's office, and the bar was mine.

The moment I stepped onto the catwalk running alongside the *Anna Grace,* I could see she had been boarded.

The starboard top lifeline was dangling near the waterline, and a life jacket lay straddling the helm.

I dropped the gym bag and pulled the Glock out of the shoulder holster. There was no wind, and the water around the boat was still. Whoever had been on the boat had probably left. Nearing the stern, I stepped out of my shoes, stripped off my socks, crouched on the edge of the catwalk, the Glock in both hands, and leaped over the lower lifeline and into the stern well.

I landed on my feet facing the bow, the gun straight in front. The boat rocked from the sudden shift in center of gravity. Anyone in the cabin would instantly have felt the presence of someone on deck.

For thirty seconds, I didn't move. I was partially concealed and protected from anyone coming out of the cabin – or firing from the top of the cabin steps – by the structures on deck. Slowly, keeping the pilothouse between me and the cabin, I eased forward, squatting on the balls of my feet like a baseball catcher, the gun held in front of me.

I made it across the cockpit to the companionway without seeing or hearing anything below.

"Slate!"

My name boomed over the docks as though the speaker had shouted it through a bullhorn. It took all the discipline I had to avoid turning my head to search for the shouter. My eyes remained locked on the companionway exit.

It helped, though, that I recognized the voice. In a moment, the speaker's shadow fell across my face, and I knew that Moeller was standing on the catwalk above me.

"Slate," he said again, not much quieter. Moeller's voice had two levels, loud and painful. "Yeah." I said it without turning my head.

"There's nobody down there, man. You can stop the cops-and-robbers shtick. I know it's fun, but, really, I already checked." He jumped down and landed lightly on the deck, came around and opened the companionway door. "See? Nobody home."

I lowered the gun to my side, mostly because Moeller was now in the line of fire. "All right," I said. "You checked. When?"

"Early this morning. I had started out to get beignets and chicory coffee at Cafe Beignets, and I saw the lifeline was down. Tried to call you but your cell phone was off. Nobody there then either, but – well – you'll see. They trashed the place."

I stepped down the companionway and peered inside.

"Trashed" is part of the contemporary argot, but it was not quite an apt description. "Searched" would've been better.

It looked as though every object in the place, including paper ones — especially including paper ones — had been picked up, looked at, then thrown to the cabin deck.

I held onto the companionway rail to avoid having to set foot on the mess.

Moeller's face appeared in the rectangle of light above me. "Sorry, my friend. I didn't want to touch anything until you had been here. Would you like some help cleaning up?"

I swung myself back up on deck. "No. I appreciate it, but this is something I have to do. How about tomorrow morning? I need to talk to you. You going to be around?"

Moeller stepped up onto the dock, did an about-face, and threw me a two-fingered salute. "You got it, Captain. See you in the morning."

Boats at anchorage are hardly the most secure homes. The marina during the day was full of good people, captains and boat hands and waitresses and fishermen and diesel mechanics who tried to watch out for each other, but most of the boats rode empty after sundown, and a sheriff's patrol car managed to drive by only once a night.

An unoccupied boat is an invitation to thieves. Boat owners know this. Smart boat owners keep little of value on their boats.

I opened the companionway and got to work.

One thing I knew for sure: the only important document on the boat was the ship's log. A boat without a log was like an airplane without logbooks. Worth something, no doubt, but worth much less than a boat with intact logs.

It was also pretty certain that the ship's log was not what the unscheduled visitors were looking for. It was equally certain that they knew more about what they were looking for than I did.

I started by picking up every single piece of paper off the cabin deck and laying them out in collated batches on the boat's table.

Warranties. Instructions for the ship's radios. The GPS manual. A manual for the ancient but functioning Loran. A couple of dozen paperback novels.

Down at the bottom of the pile, the ship's log, lying face down as though someone had held it upside down to shake it, then dropped it on the floor.

The surface of the log binder was leather and might take fingerprints. So might the companionway rail and other parts of the boat. But I didn't have a pair of evidence gloves, and every assistant prosecutor in every DA's office has had to explain to a jury, or have a witness do it, that finding identifiable fingerprints at a crime scene is rare, even when the perpetrators didn't wear gloves.

I put the logbook back in its place in the desk.

In the front drawer of the desk, I kept an ancient marine-grade laptop computer. I was about to close the drawer when I noticed that the little green "on" light on the front of the case was glowing.

I pulled the computer out of the drawer and opened the top. The screen was dark, the computer in sleep mode. I pushed the i/o button, and the screen came to life; on the right side was my name, and under it appeared the legend "1 document open."

I clicked the document button. A WordPerfect window opened to a document in which someone had typed in all caps: IF U KNOW WHAT'S GOOD FOR U STAY OUT OF THE OIL & GAS BUSNESS. The author had named the file YOU and saved it to the desktop.

I right-clicked the mouse pad to see if the writer of the note left any more electronic clues. "Reveal Codes" revealed nothing. "Properties" told me the document had been created at 4:14 a.m. on January 25. This morning, probably not long before Moeller went out for coffee and doughnuts.

After cleaning up the boat and going dockside for a sandwich and a cup of gumbo, I returned to my desk and the laptop.

I saved the note to the hard drive in both Word Perfect and rich text format and put both versions in a new folder on the desktop.

I closed Word Perfect, pulled the memory stick Akilah had given me out of my pocket, and inserted it in the USB port on the side of the case.

I clicked on the "My Computer" icon. The computer recognized the memory stick as a "removable disk" on the E-drive. I clicked again. The legend "PASSWORD: -----------------" appeared on the monitor.

I tried Kramer. Nothing. Kris. Still nothing. I tried various combinations of the family's names. I tried the three initials of Kramer's law firm: WWW. Then Woolf.

This was useless. I couldn't tell whether the files were encrypted because I couldn't get past the password protection. Did Akilah use the term encrypted when she meant password protected? Most people who knew enough about computers to use the term "encrypted" wouldn't confuse that with mere password protection. Did Akilah know the password? Had she simply forgotten to give it to me?

I realized I was staring into the depths of the notebook screen. My eyeballs felt detached from their muscles. The computer wasn't going to tell me the password.

I pulled the memory stick out of the USB port, capped it, and returned it to my pocket.

I drank a glass of water, visited the head, stripped to my underwear, then sat cross-legged on my bunk and meditated for ten minutes. I stood, stretched the knots out of my legs, and lay down.

Before I started to get drowsy, I rolled over on my side, pulled the Glock out of its holster, and placed it on the floor next to the bunk.

In the old days when Anna and David were alive, I'd kept a loaded semi-automatic on a bedside table on my side of the big four-poster bed Anna and I had shared. A loaded pistol kept in a house with a child present isn't dangerous if the owner of the pistol applies knowledge and common sense.

Trigger locks are fashionable and politically correct – if anything associated with triggers is politically correct – but clumsy, slow, and dangerous if the gun is locked and the intruder is already in the house.

The pistol on my bedside table in my other life had been a Colt's Government-model .45. I'd never left it cocked in the house.

Without a round in the chamber, that fine old gun was less dangerous than the heavy brass lamp on the bedside table. No young child – and for that matter, not so many women – possessed the grip strength to pull back the slide and cock the big Colt's. The only way a kid could hurt himself with it would have been to drop it on his toe.

And I had practiced enough to know that I could cock the gun, flip off the safety, and fire it in less than a second.

But I wasn't lying on my bed beside my wife in our four-bedroom neo-Colonial anymore. I was in a bunk on a small boat. The distance between me and the companionway hatch could be measured in two heartbeats.

For this purpose, I'd take Gaston Glock's design over Samuel Colt's any day. With a round in the chamber and no safety except the unique little pressure device on the trigger's tip, holding a Glock in your hand is like having a gun barrel in your index finger.

I slept a pleasant sleep without dreams.

CHAPTER TWELVE

Thursday January 26

Hans Moeller had grown up in Zurich. Six-two, rangy, with close-cropped blond hair and scant white eyebrows, Moeller was graduated from the Swiss Federal Institute of Technology – the same undergraduate school from which Albert Einstein was graduated sixty years earlier. Moeller, however, by his account, had been a better student. He had later invented some indispensable process or product for making clocks tick or computers compute or doodads do – he never had explained exactly what – and made a fortune or two and retired.

Now Moeller divided his time between Switzerland and his forty-three foot Cheoy Lee motor sailer. The *Billy Tell* spent its winters on the Gulf Coast, sometimes hauling charter clients to the small islands the big cruise ships couldn't touch, mostly serving as a live-aboard when Moeller wanted a break from the snow, as seemed to be the case now.

Late every April, Moeller would show up with a crew member or two or three he had collected on the slopes or in the shops of the Bahnhofstrasse – somehow always tan, female, and blonde – and they would sail around the Florida cape and slide down the Caribbean archipelago, sometimes as far as Caracas, before heading back north on the western side of the Windwards, around Cuba, and back up the intracoastal waterway or off-shore, as the mood struck him, and back to Orange Beach.

Moeller's schedule seemed backwards to me until I'd visited him in Zurich and Gstaad one January. After that it made perfect sense.

We sat in the cockpit of the *Billy Tell* just before sunrise, steaming mugs of coffee in hand, watching the dockyard begin to come to life. Moeller's boat did not have a permanent home on the Redneck Riviera. The marina considered him a seasonal visitor, and this year they had assigned him slip F-18.

"So, Slate, aside from your latest intrigue, how are things with you? Are you ready for the introductions?"

Every spring, Moeller offered to set me up with one or perhaps more of his active crew members. Every spring I told him I would let him know.

"Have you ever seen the old Burt Reynolds movie called *Smokey and the Bandit*?"

"Who is Burt Reynolds?"

"I'll accept that as a negative answer." Moeller has certain gaps in his familiarity with American popular culture. "Anyway, in that movie, or maybe it's in the sequel, the actor Burt Reynolds portrays a redneck character with a fast car who bedevils local law enforcement. In one scene, the sheriff, having stopped the car for the umpteenth time, is asking the Reynolds character whether he has any fears. 'I ain't afraid of but two things,' Reynolds says. 'What's that?' says the sheriff. 'Women and the police.'"

Moeller just nodded. Perhaps only rednecks – approximately eighteen per cent of the United States population, according to a study I read that called us "Anglo-Irish" – can appreciate this sort of humor. "And what do you fear, Slate?"

"Those are a subset of the one set of entities in the universe worthy of anyone's fear – *homo sapiens*."

"Fearsome creatures."

"And you, my friend?"

He swept his arm about in a broad gesture that took in the entire marina. "That it is all going to end badly in the none-too-distant future."

"Not the asteroids again." Among Moeller's hobbies was tracking near-earth objects using a rooftop observatory at his chalet in the Alps and a computer program he had written.

"No, my friend. The odds of a catastrophic strike are long except on a very distant time frame. Earth is three-quarters water, and most of the land mass is uninhabited. Though I'd feel better about my calculations if we had identified all the objects in the asteroid belt and if we didn't keep losing track of the ones we've already found. No, this scenario, I'm afraid, carries a much higher probability."

He sipped his coffee. "I came back to the States directly from a meeting with my bankers in Zurich."

"That's something I will never be able to say."

"No. Not anymore, not after your government's pursuit of UBS and enactment of a law requiring foreign banks to provide information to the IRS prompted the Swiss banks to cease offering accounts to U.S. citizens. But you can still benefit from my bankers' advice."

"Which is?"

"Prepare."

"For?"

"Economic collapse. Financial Armageddon. The coming New Dark Ages." Moeller smiled. "Being Swiss bankers, of course they don't use those terms. Nevertheless, what they say is that this time, it really is different. What's happening in the Eurozone because of the debts run up by the peripheral economies is just the overture. The larger economies, particularly the United States and Japan, have finally amassed so much debt that the Keynesian techniques the central bankers used during most of the twentieth century are no longer available."

"Well, Japan has that demographic problem."

"Yes, forty years from now Japan's population will be thirty per cent smaller than it is now. That problem for now is unique to Japan – it comes later for China, but China will suffer from its own demographic bomb about mid-century – but it's still significant because Japan is the world's third largest economy. And it has the world's largest sovereign debt. But I digress."

"Go on then."

"In the past, reserve banks used money creation and low interest rates to accelerate growth out of a recession. But this recession is the deepest since the Great Depression, and it's not just a growth recession. It's an asset deflation recession. In the United States, the Fed has expanded its balance sheet with risky assets and used what my bankers call ZIRP – the Zero Interest Rate Policy."

"Bankers enjoy their acronyms almost as much as geeks do."

"Bankers are geeks. At least, Swiss bankers are. I don't believe you could say that about, say, Atlanta bankers, or even the so-called investment bankers at the likes of Goldman Sachs. The investment banks do keep a few pet geeks about, though.

"Anyway, the ZIRP and the bond purchases have done little good except for the beginnings of a stock market bubble and the continuation of the Treasury bond bubble. Banks don't want to make risky loans, and the contraction of real estate prices reduced loan demand. But at some point, one of two things will happen. The Fed will decide it has to end its bond purchases and the ZIRP policy, or the markets, fearing inflation caused by all the money the Fed has printed, or maybe in the face of actual inflation, will take the ZIRP out of the Fed's hands. Either way, interest rates will rise."

"Okay. So what happens then?"

"Game over, my friend. In the past, the Fed could subdue inflation by raising interest rates. Paul Volcker, when he was Fed chairman back in the eighties, is the meta-example. He raised the federal funds rate up to twenty per cent. My bankers think that without Volcker the United States might have shot into hyperinflation back then.

"But now the huge U.S. debt creates a ceiling on the Fed's ability to raise interest rates. At some point on the interest rate curve, neither the United States nor Japan will be able to pay the interest on their debt. So if the Fed fails to raise interest rates as Volcker did, they risk hyperinflation. And if the Fed were to raise interest rates Volcker-style, at some point the U.S. and Japan will be unable to afford interest payments.

"Either way, the dollar and the yen will collapse, the world will have to invent a new reserve currency, and the United States will no longer be a worldwide empire."

"There's a silver lining in there somewhere."

"Yes, Slate, but not for most U.S. citizens. For them a standard of living maybe eighty per cent lower is their destiny sometime in this century."

"What's the solution?"

"For me? No dollar or yen-denominated assets. Not a problem for a Swiss. For you? Not so easy. If you can, own other currencies and hard assets. Gold."

"Somehow I knew you'd eventually utter that four-letter word."

He shrugged. "I'm Swiss. The Swiss appreciate gold because it's politically neutral. Like us."

The sun began to peek over the horizon toward the Perdido Pass, where the Perdido bridge connected Alabama Point to Florida Point and divided the panhandle between Alabama to the west and Florida to the east. The rising sun streaked the sky in oranges and yellows and seemed to mock the apocalyptic vision of the gloomy Bahnhofstrasse bankers Moeller had related. See? I'm still rising every morning, it said.

"So, what's this business with your boat all about?" Moeller asked.

"Not sure yet. If I gave you some encrypted files on a computer disk, could you decrypt them?"

"Depends. What type of encryption? How robust?"

"I don't know. I don't even know for sure that they're encrypted. The files are on a thumb drive. You can't get to the files without a password."

"You don't have the password?"

"No."

"Then why do you think the files are encrypted?"

"The person who gave me the memory stick said so."

"Does this have anything do to with the visit to your boat?"

I nodded. "Probably." I gave Moeller a sketch of the Kramer case. I left out the message typed on my laptop.

Moeller was silent for a couple of minutes. A gull flew over the boat and settled on top of a light pole at the end of the catwalk that ran alongside Moeller's boat slip.

The bird regarded us sleepily. Hoping to steal some food, no doubt, but not energetic enough to try.

"How did the soccer goalie – Akilah? – how did she know the files were encrypted if they are password-protected?"

"I don't know. I don't even know whether she mixed up the terms."

"The possibilities are: first, the Kramer girl told her the files were encrypted. Second, the Kramer girl told her the password, and she opened the folder but discovered the files were encrypted."

"She told me the files were encrypted."

Moeller ignored me. "Third, Akilah knows the decryption code and the password. Fourth. . . ."

"She knows what's in the files."

"Right you are, Mr. Slate. And they say people from Alabama are dumb."

"Sometimes that observation is correct."

Moeller squinted across the rim of his coffee cup. A slice of the sun had just appeared over the horizon in his line of sight through the forest of masts in the docks. "Slate."

"Yes."

"Give me the thumb drive. I will run the password prompt through a brute-force password cracker I have on my computer here in the boat. If we get lucky, that will give us access to the files, but they may still have to be decrypted."

The thumb drive was in my pants pocket. I handed it to Moeller and returned to my boat.

I spent the rest of the morning doing a few of the endless chores of sailboat maintenance and second-guessing my decision to ask Moeller to spend time with the thumb drive. I needed to get back to Birmingham. And I needed a long talk with the goalkeeper for the Alabama Southern women's soccer team.

CHAPTER THIRTEEN

Moeller's password program was not a success. With more time, he told me, he was sure it would work. For reasons clear to both of us, though, I could not leave the device with him, and he reluctantly returned it.

After a quick lunch, seafood gumbo, cole slaw, saltine crackers, and iced tea, at Hemingway's, I packed the Escort with more clothes, the laptop, and, this time, my little Ruger LCP, a potent gun about the size of a cellphone that clicked into the Fobus holster strapped to my ankle.

I swapped the Glock .45 for my older Glock, the model 17. The model number of the Glock pistol referred to the magazine capacity. With seventeen rounds in the magazine of the Glock, I hoped not to need the Ruger.

But if I did need it, I wanted it, full magazine inserted, on my ankle, not in the locker in my boat.

At the WalMart in Orange Beach, I bought two boxes of ammunition, a six pack of lemon-flavored bottled water, and spare flashlight batteries.

I got back in the Escort and drove to the airport, through the gate and onto the ramp, and parked the car in front of my hangar.

I transferred my stuff to the Albatros and drove the courtesy car back to its usual parking spot behind the FBO office. When I tossed the keys to the girl at the counter, she gave me some grief for keeping the courtesy car overnight.

Somehow I doubted that the occupants of the new Falcon on the ramp missed the Escort much.

The Southeastern weather was holding, with a cold wedge of higher-pressure air pushing away the rain a little longer. I could avoid filing IFR and to save time decided not to file a VFR flight plan.

VFR flight plans serve one purpose – to allow Air Force and Civil Air Patrol teams to make informed decisions regarding search and res-cue after a crash. I would remain in contact with air traffic control facili-ties throughout the flight, mooting any need for a flight plan.

In Birmingham I picked up another rental and drove to the Tutwiler. I spent only enough time there to transfer my bags and see if anyone besides the maid had been in the room.

The hotel room safe no longer seemed the most secure option for the memory stick or the handwritten notes.

Down in the lobby, I told the concierge that I needed to place a cou-ple of items in the hotel safe. The day concierge, a chunky but efficient-looking woman in her mid-forties, took my five-dollar tip and led me through a warren of offices and corridors behind the front desk to an ele-vator just large enough for two. We descended slowly to the basement.

The elevator door opened on a scene out of the 1950s.

In a large room floored in peeling gray linoleum sat a dozen metal and glass cubicles. I could see the heads of workers in a few.

At one end of the room, the concierge opened a door to a small room no larger than a walk-in closet. The concierge smiled slightly, stepped into the room, and closed the door.

Fifteen seconds later, the door swung open, and the concierge motioned me in. Inside the room, taking up essentially the entire space, sat a combination safe with peeling beige paint. The safe door was open. Lining the safe were perhaps a hundred lockboxes of various sizes. The concierge opened a box and left the key in the lock.

I removed the memory stick from my pants pocket and the notes from my jacket and placed them inside the box. The concierge closed the box and handed me the key.

"You're all set," she said. "Box number is on the key." She pointed to the key.

"Right," I said and followed her back to the lobby.

In the car on I-65 South on the way to Alabama Southern, I called Sally Kronenberg's office but got a recording. I didn't leave a message.

I didn't want to have to go through Miller to speak with Akilah, but without the coach I wasn't sure how to find the girl. I'd just have to do what I usually did – figure it out as I went along.

At the campus gate, I got lucky. The guard on duty recognized me and had apparently decided I was harmless. He nodded as I coasted by.

I drove to the athletic complex and parked out front.

If Akilah knew the password and the encryption key, I'd have to convince her to give them to me. Both seemed unlikely; why would she give me the drive without the keys to the information?

And, whether she'd opened the document or not, the people who'd left the message on my laptop might figure out or force Kris to tell them that she'd given Akilah the memory stick. Akilah might be in danger.

Today the athletic complex was humming. On the ground floor through tall glass windows, I could see trainers working with a dozen or so male athletes in the weight room. In the lobby a couple of young women, probably athletes on partial scholarships, were giving a tour to a busload of high-school kids.

Upstairs, the small anteroom outside the coach's office was occupied this time. The young woman at the desk had the shoulders of a swimmer. "Help you?" she asked.

I gave her my best smile. "Only if you can tell me where I can find Coach Kronenberg."

"Are you Mr. Slate?" she said.

"How did you know? Did I forget to take the name tag off my jacket?"

"Hi, Mr. Slate. I'm Alison. Coach K described you. And she told me to come find her if you came by. She's down on the soccer field. Do you know where it is? Just behind the building?"

"I've seen it. Thanks, Alison."

"No problem."

Sally Kronenberg wore sweats, an elastic band with an athletic shoe logo holding back her hair. She stood in front of a portable soccer goal on the practice field.

Nine girls, most of them in shorts and sweatshirts with the Alabama Southern logo on the front, were lined up fifteen yards in front of the goal. As each girl came to the front of the line, a student assistant surrounded by soccer balls rolled one out, and the player rocketed the ball toward the goal.

Each player got three kicks. I watched all twelve have a turn. The coach didn't stop every shot. But she didn't miss many either.

When the penalty-kick drill was over, the players moved on to passing drills, and Sally Kronenberg walked over to me. "Hi," she said. "How long have you been watching?"

"Long enough," I told her.

"Long enough to see I'm not the age of these girls anymore. Normally one of our goalkeepers would stay in goal for that drill, but Akilah is not here today, and – you know about Kris."

"Do you know why Akilah didn't show?"

"No. I haven't heard from her."

"Is that unusual?"

"Yeah. A little, for Akilah especially, but these are voluntary workouts. It's offseason."

"If it's possible, I need to speak with Akilah again."

"What's up?"

I outlined the events at the marina but left out the memory stick and the encryption.

"All right," she said. "Let's go find her. I hope you don't mind if I shower first."

I followed Sally Kronenberg into the sports complex and waited for her in the lobby in an overstuffed chair.

The high-school kids had completed their tour. I closed my eyes and tried to focus on my breath while I recalled some of the details in the materials Kramer had left with me.

Most of the documents were from the fraudulent oil lease files Kramer worked as assistant AG. Some of the names on the files were familiar: Monetto, Brunini, Marcello.

Stuffed in an unmarked file folder in the back of the document case were clippings from a recently notorious punitive damages case, *State of Alabama v. ExxonMobil*. In *ExxonMobil*, the state had alleged, and ultimately proved to a jury, that Exxon was underreporting its take from offshore gas wells to reduce the royalties it was obliged to pay to the Alabama government.

As usual in these cases, the three-and-half-billion-dollar punitive damages award enjoyed wide coverage in the media. The Alabama Supreme Court's reversal of the award merited fifteen seconds on CNBC and a two-inch AP story buried deep the pages of the newspapers that bothered to print it.

A law firm in Mobile had represented the state in the ExxonMobil case. Nothing in the file indicated Kramer's law firm participated.

And I'd found precious little to connect the old files to the present.

Sally Kronenberg came down to the lobby in a gray wool skirt, red silk blouse, and a gray wool blazer. She wore black pumps and one thick gold chain around her neck. She carried a black raincoat over her arm.

My eyes must have told her I'd noticed.

She shrugged. "I'm going out tonight. Dinner. Then a basketball game on campus."

"I didn't say a word."

"You didn't have to." She smiled a little, one corner of her mouth turning up.

"Well, listen, if you don't have time for this, you don't have to help me do my job."

"No, it's still early. The game is not until seven-thirty."

She shrugged again. "Well. I don't know where to start to look for Akilah any more than you do. I'm sure she's fine. I called her cell phone from my office, but I just got her voice mail. I left a message and asked her to call. In the meantime, I suppose we could check her dorm. But it's getting close to time for the athletes to have supper. They eat together in the dining hall at the dorm quadrangle, most nights."

"So we should check there first."

The coach nodded. "Right. If she's not there we can check her room."

We pushed through the doors of the athletic complex. "I have to lock up," she said. "We're the last to leave."

She produced a key, locked the front door, and turned to gesture toward the sidewalk paralleling the building. "We can walk," she said. "It's always faster than driving here. It's near the coffee shop where we were before."

Inside the dining room, Coach Kronenberg approached two tables of boisterous girls eating pizza.

I hung back at the entrance, but one sweep of the room told me that Akilah Ziyenge wasn't dining with her fellow athletes tonight.

Several students glanced toward me. Somehow I didn't think they mistook me for a student.

After a couple of minutes, Sally Kronenberg came back to where I was standing. "They don't know where she is. A couple of girls thought she might be cramming for an exam in her room. The dorm is just outside and around the corner. Let's go."

On the way, the coach glanced sideways at me and smirked. "One of the girls asked if you were my date."

"Too bad I'm not," I said without thinking.

"Think so?"

I shook my head. "Sorry. Not really."

"Another girl said you were better looking than the guy they saw me with last time."

"You do have intelligent athletes here, don't you?"

"We try."

"So, am I?"

"Are you what?"

"Is she right?"

"Hmm. Maybe." She smiled and looked at me sideways again. "Maybe so."

Coach Kronenberg waved her faculty identification card in front of a sensor to unlock the front door at the red brick three-story dorm. Inside, a young man wearing some type of identification card on a chain around his neck stepped out of the hall advisor's office. He recognized Coach Kronenberg but gave me a hard look. He was a kid and hadn't practiced as long as I had, so he had to look back at the coach.

"Can I help you?" he said.

"We need to go up to see Akilah Ziyenge," Coach Kronenberg told him.

"Sure, you can go on up, Coach," said the kid. "For what it's worth, I haven't seen her all day. But, uh, who's he?" He indicated me with a small movement of his head.

"My name is Slate," I said.

"Just Slate?"

"Mr. Slate."

Coach Kronenberg shook her head. *Mister* Slate is with me. He's — he's working with the police on a matter involving a student here."

The kid looked skeptical, but he was out of his weight class. "Well sure, Coach, y'all can both go on up. Say hello for me."

The suite, 316, was on the third floor. The elevator opened onto a long narrow corridor. 316 was one door from the north end.

Coach Kronenberg knocked on the door to 316. There was no answer.

I reached around her and knocked, harder. Again, there was no response.

Coach Kronenberg turned the doorknob, and the door opened.

She looked at me. "I guess the girls sometimes leave these doors unlocked," she said.

The door opened into a sitting room about fifteen feet square. Inside I could see a couch, a couple of armchairs, an entertainment center with a music system and a big Sony monitor. The walls were decorated with black and white movie posters.

Through an open doorway at the back of the living space was a kitchenette. A small plate with a sandwich crust sat on the counter. To the left, through an open door, was a small neat bedroom, unoccupied, lights off.

"I'm not sure which one," Coach Kronenberg said. "Akilah?" she called. "It's Coach Kronenberg. Akilah?"

The suite was silent. Sally turned to me. "I guess she isn't here."

"Since we are here, let's make sure," I said. I crossed the sitting room and knocked on the closed door on my right. Again, no sound. I opened the door.

This room was almost identical to the room on the left. Neat and clean. The lights were off. The walls were covered with soccer posters, some of them twins to the posters I'd seen in Kris Kramer's room at her parents' home.

But here there was one difference.

In this room, in the half-light from the common room, Akilah Ziyenge lay face down on her neat bed.

An African savannah motif graced the bedspread. The young woman's feet were bare. She was wearing gray cotton sweat pants and a black sports bra. The unstudied disarray of her limbs and the utter stillness in the room provided me with information I didn't want but knew I must absorb in every detail: Akilah Ziyenge was dead.

CHAPTER FOURTEEN

I heard one sharp intake of breath at my shoulder. Sally Kronenberg pushed past me and stepped over to the body to feel for a carotid pulse.

She looked at me and shook her head, then held up her hand for me to see. A small smear of blood streaked her first two fingers.

I moved to her side and looked at Akilah's neck without touching the body. I could just see the edge of what appeared to be strangulation or ligature marks.

Sally slipped her hand beneath my arm and pulled me close. "You have to get them," she whispered, the sound of her voice sibilant and eerie in this close room of death. "Promise me," she said. "Make them pay for this."

I looked down into her eyes and nodded. "Whatever it takes," I said.

The coach released my arm.

"We have to call the police," I told her

"Campus or city?" she said, now using her normal voice.

"City. I should call Leon Grubbs first."

"But we're on campus. Wouldn't the campus police have jurisdiction?"

"I don't really care about the campus police. I'm calling Grubbs."

"But I'm on staff here. I think I have to call the campus police."

I could see her point. "Look, this shouldn't be so tough. We both have cell phones. Let me call Grubbs first. When I'm done, you make your call."

"Got it. Go ahead and call now. I'm going back downstairs and talk to the student in the residence hall office."

This was my turn to take her arm. "Coach – Sally – no. Let me take any heat from the police. Your campus police chief is not going to be happy with you for being here with me. You don't need to be accused of interfering with an investigation. Let the police talk to the kid. Go out and sit in the common room. I'll call Grubbs now. You call the campus police as soon as I'm off. That will give me a little time to look around."

She shook her head sharply and took a deep breath. "I'm sure you're right." She sighed again. "Damn."

When I asked for Leon Grubbs at the homicide unit, the officer who answered put me on hold.

Searching the tiny dorm room wouldn't take long. Nothing seemed askew.

Textbooks and a dictionary were arranged neatly between simple wooden bookends on the study desk under the window. The shade on the small lamp on the desk was straight. A laundry basket in the closet held a few items of clothing, and blouses and dresses hung on hangers, with jeans and sweaters in organized stacks on a shelf above the rod.

Either Akilah had died without much of a struggle, which seemed unlikely for a healthy, strong athlete, or the killer or killers had straightened the room after she was dead.

I returned to the desk and tried to focus on my breath while I observed each object. The lamp, of cheap plastic, might have been part of the furnishings provided by the college. The desk was an inexpensive wood laminate.

Centered over the kneehole sat an HP notebook computer, the screen with its upside-down logo closed, the power and on/off lights dark. I'd noticed the computer a moment ago but had not observed it with a still mind.

Of course, I'd missed something obvious. Front and center below the dark light bar, a four-inch hole appeared. Someone – the killer? – had popped out the computer's hard drive.

After two minutes, a police lieutenant I didn't know picked up a handset and identified himself as the night watch commander. I got off the phone with him and tried Grubbs' cell. He answered after four rings. "This better be important, Slate," he said.

"It is."

He listened without interruption while I told him where I was and what I'd seen. When I'd finished, Grubbs said, "Things were going pretty well for me before you flew back into town, you know that? Is this connected to Kramer?"

"That would be my guess."

He said, "I'll be there as soon as I can, but I have to work through the campus police. Have they been informed?"

I told him that Sally Kronenberg would make that call. "One other thing," I said. "Send along some techies with computer skills." I told him about the missing hard drive.

"We'll log it in as evidence. We don't need those guys at a murder scene. Have the lady make the call to campus security now. And Slate? Don't move or touch anything. Understand?"

"Yes, sir, understood," I said, and pushed the End button.

I stepped out into the common area where Sally Kronenberg had heard my call end and was already on her cell phone calling campus security.

The campus was small. I had maybe two minutes.

In Akilah Ziyenge's trash can at the end of her desk was a balled-up plastic grocery bag. I pulled the bag out, slipped it over my hand, and opened every drawer in the girl's desk. Notebook hard drives are about the size of the adult human palm, but that's large enough to see at a glance if they have been placed in a desk drawer.

The missing hard drive was not in the desk, and I saw nothing else other than the usual pens, stamps, and paperclips.

I hadn't seen a computer bag in the room earlier, and I didn't see one now. No other place in the room made sense. Under the mattress? I couldn't look there, not now.

I stripped the bag off my hand and returned it where I'd found it just as loud male voices and heavy footsteps, a staccato squadron of them, sounded in the hall.

The common room door opened, and Director of Campus Security John Miller strode in at the front of the group. Three uniformed campus police officers in full gear were a step behind. Miller was still in his Brooks Brothers suit.

"I still don't understand what he's doing here," Miller said to Sally Kronenberg.

"I told you, John – Chief. Kris Kramer's father hired Slate to help find Kris. Anything I can do to help Kris and that family, I'll do. I don't care if I have to break some rule."

Miller made a noise like he needed to clear his throat. "Later."

He turned to the police officers behind him. "Secure the scene. Don't go into the room. Don't touch anything." The officers got to work with crime tape. They pulled on latex gloves before touching doorknobs.

Miller spoke again to the soccer coach. "We don't have the resources to conduct a murder investigation on our own. We know our limitations. I already called Birmingham Homicide. Their investigators are on the way." He turned to me for the first time. "Did you touch anything in the room?"

I shook my head. "No. I opened the door and found her. Neither of us touched anything in there except for the coach checking for a pulse."

Miller nodded. "My officers will stay here. I want you two to come downstairs with me, to the dormitory office. You're going to have a long night."

Director of Campus Security Miller was wrong. Not long after Leon Grubbs arrived with his investigators, he took me aside. "Look, I don't need you here," he said.

"I can stay as long as you want me. Miller already told me my night would be long."

"You don't understand," Grubbs said. "Miller is not exactly playing ball here." He glanced in Miller's direction. "The mind games may stop if you're not here. I know what I need from you, and I know where to find you. I'll call you in the morning. Meantime, you do your job, I'll do mine."

I didn't need to be told twice. Miller had Sally Kronenberg cornered.

It was not an evening for the social graces. I left the campus without saying goodbye.

CHAPTER FIFTEEN

Friday January 27

Leon Grubbs didn't call. But then, he hadn't said I promise.

The morning wasn't a total loss. I showered, meditated for thirty minutes, and enjoyed the excellent cheese omelette in the Tutwiler restaurant.

As I finished, Susan Kramer called my cell phone. She wanted to talk. That made two of us.

Before getting in the car, I went back to the room and called hotel security. I needed to have the thumb drive with me in case someone I spoke with during the day, whether Susan Kramer or her son or someone else, could tell me how to access its contents.

Downtown Birmingham traffic was like morning traffic in every city, but I made it to Mountain Brook by nine. This time the Kramer boy, Paul, allowed me entrance and escorted me to the library. I was making some kind of progress.

Susan Kramer was dressed in a gray tweed business suit with a single strand of pearls and matching pearl earrings. She stood and extended her hand. "Mr. Slate," she said.

"It's just Slate, I think, Mom." The boy looked at me. "Isn't that right?"

"That's correct. Just Slate."

Susan Kramer said, "Well. Slate. Please sit down."

Susan Kramer and her son sat at opposite ends of the red sofa covered in silk fabric. Today I noticed it wasn't actually solid red; a subtle gold leaf motif had been woven into the red background. I sat across from them in a wing chair with tufted gold fabric.

"Thank you for attending my husband's service, Mr. Slate. Paul is taking a few days off from school during this difficult time for our family. I cannot believe how far this thing, whatever it is, has unraveled. Kris's roommate Akilah's murder is all over the news. So sad. Such a fine, lovely girl. So tragic."

I nodded. "Yes."

She took a deep breath. "Now. Don hired you to find our daughter. Isn't that right?"

"Yes, ma'am."

Her nostrils flared slightly as she took in a lungful of air and straightened her back. "Then let's get to work."

She asked me what I knew. I told her.

She asked if I thought her daughter's disappearance had anything to do with her husband's work. I said that her husband seemed to think so, but I didn't know.

I told her about the thumb drive without mentioning how I'd come into possession of it. Both she and her son said they knew nothing about it.

Paul Kramer asked the question I'd been asking myself. Were his father's death and his sister's disappearance connected with Akilah's death? I told him that was a reasonable conclusion. What I didn't have was proof.

Susan Kramer spoke again. "So. A reasonable assumption is that my husband's death and my daughter's – disappearance – are both connected to my husband's work, possibly to a single legal matter. Is that correct?"

I told her those were reasonable working theories.

Susan Kramer stood. "Then we are meeting in the wrong place. I have a law degree and practiced for two years before I married Don. But I know nothing about my husband's work. We both preferred things that way. Anyway, lawyers have that thing about confidentiality. So we need to speak with my husband's law partners. Immediately. Paul and I will drive in my car. You know the way, don't you, uh, Slate?"

I said I did.

"Let's go," she said.

I told her that it might be more efficient if they were expecting us.

She looked at me as though she were having second thoughts about keeping me on staff. "I intend to call Bill Woolf on my cell while I'm driving in. They'd better make time for me," she said.

They did make time for us, and, indeed, most of "them" were in the office, including a few legal assistants and paralegals.

Susan Kramer, and, perforce, her son Paul and I, were not kept waiting in the lobby.

Woolf's assistant bustled out to show us into a small conference room near Woolf's office. An assistant served coffee.

Woolf appeared in the doorway before I'd finished stirring. He gave Susan Kramer a hug and sat at one end of the table. Susan and Paul Kramer took chairs immediately to his right. I sat at the opposite end.

"Susan, how can we help you?" Woolf began.

"You can start by giving Mr. Slate access to every file Don was working on. Slate . . . Mr. Slate thinks Kris's situation and Don's, uh, Don's death may be related."

Meeting first Susan's eyes, then mine, Woolf nodded slightly several times. "Right," he said finally. "I can see the point here. But our files are privileged. Slate, you're a lawyer; Susan, you have a law degree. You both understand."

I nodded back. It was contagious as a yawn. "I do understand your issues. But those files may help solve a murder and Kris's disappearance. I need them, and I think you understand that, don't you, Bill Woolf?"

The files might help solve two murders, but I didn't want to bring last night into the conversation unless I had to.

"Yes," he said. He turned to Susan Kramer. "Would you all excuse me for a moment?" He wheeled around in his chair, stood, and in one stride opened the door and disappeared, closing the door behind him.

Susan Kramer turned to me. "What was that about?" she said.

"No idea," I said.

Susan Kramer looked down at the table, and her shoulders began to shake. She wasn't holding it together as thoroughly as it appeared.

Paul took his mother's hand. Her jaw muscles were visible, her mouth a thin line. I picked up my coffee mug, said something about looking for Woolf, and went out into the hall through the door at my end of the conference room.

Down the hall in Woolf's office I found Woolf at his desk and another, older man, balding and rumpled, in one of the chairs opposite Woolf.

As I peered in the door, Woolf glanced up and saw me. "Come in, Slate, and close the door," he said.

As I did so, the other man stood, approached me, and held out his hand. "George Hill," he said.

"Sit down, Slate," Woolf said. "George is Of Counsel here and serves as my in-house ethicist. Keeps us out of trouble. George and I have been discussing these matters involving Don Kramer. We think we have a solution," he said. "Right, George?"

Hill turned to acknowledge me with a slight smile. "Yes, I see no problem with making the offer."

Woolf looked at me. "Slate, your law license is current. I had someone check. How would you feel about becoming Of Counsel to the firm on an interim basis?"

"On an interim basis?" Inane, but I had to stall while I thought.

"Just until you complete your investigation," Hill said.

I started to shake my head. "I suppose it solves your ethics issues, but it might not solve mine," I said.

"How so?" said Woolf.

"I don't need or want responsibility for, or, more precisely, to take on ethical duties to, your clients."

"Understood."

"Or to the members and associates of your firm."

"How so?" Hill asked.

"Well, not to spell it out, but if it turns out that one of the firm's clients or someone here had anything to do with Kris's disappearance or Don Kramer's murder, don't expect to invoke any privileges."

Woolf nodded. "I sincerely do not believe that anyone here would have harmed Kris or Don. Nor any of our clients. But we can craft some sort of agreement that addresses these problems. That's what we have lawyers for, right?"

He turned to Hill. "Let's get one of the transaction lawyers on this straightaway. Maybe Thornton." He stood and extended a hand. "Welcome aboard, Slate. Let's go speak with Mrs. Kramer."

The agreement drafted by Carrie Thornton, a thirty-something junior partner in the firm's transaction department with chin-length dark hair and the body of a maturing starlet, excluded me from any knowledge of or access to the firm's files except for any files Don Kramer had billed on since his tenure at the firm began.

This language created the "Chinese wall," often used by law firms when they hire lawyers from other firms that have represented clients with interests adverse to those of clients of the hiring firm. Our arrangement presented an unusual use of the Chinese wall concept, but it would have to suffice.

The contract did not mention compensation except to parrot the language commonly appearing in sales contracts: "Ten dollars and other good and valuable consideration." I planned to ask for my ten bucks in cash.

The contract did not approach perfection. We all knew that. But at least it gave me access to what I needed.

Among other things, I didn't think an agreement between a law firm and a lawyer could erase the attorney-client privilege, but since I had no intention of protecting the guilty, I didn't care.

I signed in the presence of Thornton and Woolf's assistant. Woolf signed. We went back to the conference room and explained to Susan Kramer what we had done. She had composed herself and said she was pleased I would have access to the files.

I told her we would talk later, and she and Paul left.

I had work to do.

CHAPTER SIXTEEN

Woolf White did not give me a corner office.

They didn't give me Kramer's former office, either. Instead, I got an ancient desk with a linoleum top in a corner of the file room, where I waited while a runner wheeled in boxes of files and stacked them in my vicinity.

One group of file boxes bore on their sides the label Oil & Gas Well Litigation in heavy black lettering.

It didn't require a Philadelphia lawyer to confirm, through the contents of these files, what I had guessed when I reviewed the files Kramer gave me – that Kramer had been working on a possible class action lawsuit on behalf of Alabama landowners who claimed certain oil companies had underpaid gas royalties through under-measuring and through overpayments to affiliates for marketing, gathering, compressing, and transporting gas, for deducting unrelated expenses, deducting gas that was diverted to their own use, and "producing condensate that was sold to third parties but failing to report such sales and pay royalties on those sales."

I knew nothing of the facts, but I did know enough law to appreciate the elegance of a simple breach of contract action brought on behalf of a class of plaintiffs with identical contracts and against a group of defendants as toxic, in the public's view, as oil companies.

The case should pose little difficulty on the merits, or no more than any other good plaintiffs' case, though I knew the defendants would argue that class certification would be inappropriate because audits of each well would have to be performed, and, in the jargon of class actions, individual issues would predominate over common issues, thereby precluding class certification.

But even in the absence of class certification, the cases were probably, nevertheless, worth pursuing on an individual, plaintiff-by-plaintiff basis. Pursued one-by-one or as a class, the legal fees could run into millions of dollars, even though most of these oil and gas companies were miles below the majors in size and scope of operations.

In one subfolder were DVDs with labels referenced to the paper files I had already seen.

I chose one at random and slid it into the drive of the desktop computer that appeared to be shared by everyone with file room access. The contents were what I expected – a list of .pdf files, all accessible, no encryption. Standard law firm practice.

I ejected the disk and pulled the thumb drive Kris had entrusted to her friend Akilah out of my pocket. I plugged the stick into the USB port and clicked on the icon that appeared on the monitor. The login and password screen appeared.

In the top desk drawer, I found a list of law firm employees with extensions. I picked up the phone and punched in the extension of Woolf's legal assistant. In another age, I would have thought of her as a secretary.

"Mrs. Richards," she said, her voice a half-question.

"Hi, this is Slate, down in the file room. I have a little situation here. Would you see if Don Kramer's paralegal could help me for a few minutes?"

"I think Amber is just going through Mr. Kramer's other files. I will ask her to join you right away, Mr. Slate."

A few minutes later, while I looked through the paper version of the Notes file, a heavy young woman with short black hair and no makeup appeared from the other side of my stack of file boxes. "Mr. Slate?" she said.

I stood. "Just Slate," I said.

She nodded. "I'm Amber. I'm – I was Mr. Kramer's paralegal. May I help you with something?"

"I hope so, Amber. Did you know Mr. Kramer's logins and passwords?"

"You mean the server login? We all have our own login name and password for the server. I wouldn't have needed to know his. I have my own. But for most of us, the login is just the first initial and last name. Mine is ALand. Land is my last name. So Mr. Kramer's login was probably DKramer."

"I don't know whether that's what I need." I pointed to the thumb drive. "To access the files on this device, I need a login and password."

"I probably can't help you with that, Mr. – Slate. Where did the thumb drive come from?"

I pointed – ambiguously, I hoped – to the Oil & Gas file. Amber shrugged. "That drive could have some documents on it, or it could be a draft pleading that Mr. Kramer worked on from home or on the road. Hard to say. You may want to talk to one of the IT guys. Let me see if Jacks can help you."

"Jacks," a tall blond man in his late twenties with spiky hair and heavy glasses, whose actual name, he admitted, was Michael Jackson, held network administrator privileges for the firm's computer systems and, therefore, had access to every Woolf White employee's login and password information.

Jacks worked on the computer while I read through a file of notes on under-measurement of natural gas production, but after fifteen minutes he looked over at me and shook his head.

"I've tried every combination of login id's and passwords I can come up with," he said. "Are you sure this came from a file of ours?"

I told Jacks I might have gotten the drive confused with another case, thanked him for the effort, and sat back down at the desk with the Notes file.

By five-thirty my brain was moving like syrup in the winter, and I needed a break. I picked up the phone on the desk, swallowed hard, punched 9 for an outside line, and called Sally Kronenberg's cell phone number.

"Hey!" she answered.

"Hey yourself," I said.

"Oh. Hello. Who is this?"

"It's Slate. Were you expecting someone?"

"Oh, hi. No, I just, I thought for a second it was someone else."

"Well. I've been elbows deep in documents for hours, and I need some air. Would you like to have dinner with me?"

"Hmm. Yes, but on one condition."

"What's that?"

"Allow me to choose the restaurant and make the reservations."

"You got it. Just text me the when and where."

"Will do. Thanks, Slate."

I straightened the documents on my desk before walking out to the elevator lobby, out of the building and down the street to the Tutwiler to get ready for dinner.

CHAPTER SEVENTEEN

Ninety minutes later, I sat at a tiny marble-topped table in the bar at Highlands Bar & Grill, nursing a Rob Roy and waiting for Ms. Kronenberg.

Around me a well-dressed and well-watered portion of the membership of the Birmingham Bar Association, sprinkled, no doubt, with real estate brokers, investment advisors, and a CPA or two, exchanged war stories and eyed the young women who clustered in twos and threes, bright and lively as small songbirds.

Through the glass partition separating the bar from the restaurant, diners studied menus and exchanged nods of pleasure at the food placed before them.

I watched out the window as Sally Kronenberg stepped out of a Jaguar XK8 and tossed the keys to one of the valet parking attendants. She wore a beige silk dress that flowed around her body like wings, matching stilletos on her feet, in her hand a small bag that looked as though it might be worth a month's rent.

A Skate and expensive clothes on the salary of a small college women's soccer coach; this woman could surprise me.

I picked up my drink and moved toward the maitre d's stand as Sally entered through the restaurant door. I overheard the maitre d' address her before she spoke. "Ms. Kronenberg, it's a pleasure to see you again. Will you be meeting someone for dinner this evening?"

"Yes, George, the gentleman standing just behind you."

The maitre d' turned, gave me a quick once-over, then raised his chin a fraction.

"Good enough for her?"

"You'll do, sir." He managed only the slightest smile. "Follow me please."

We sat at a table near the back. The plaster walls, hung with French bistro posters, were painted in an ocher so light it looked more like a wash than paint.

I ordered another drink. Sally Kronenberg ordered a Grey Goose martini, up, lemon twist.

I swallowed the last drops of my first Rob Roy. "So, tell me again, how did you manage to get us reservations here?"

She shrugged. "I know a guy."

"The maitre d'."

"Yes, well, George too, but I know Frank and Pardis Stitt a little."

"The owners."

She nodded. "Yes."

The waiter returned with her martini and my second Rob Roy. She picked up her glass by the stem. "Better days."

"And all our yesterdays."

We clinked glasses; our eyes met until we both looked away at other diners, the walls, the waiters. I thought I'd seen a glimmer of moisture in hers, but when I looked back, it could have been a reflection from her glass.

Our waiter saved us from more eye contact by swooping in and recommending the stone-ground baked grits for an appetizer. Sally ordered the grits; I went with the fried quail imported from Georgia, accompanied by a scrambled egg salad with spinach and bacon vinaigrette.

The description reminded me of my mother making a salad for me when I was maybe ten with fresh spinach drizzled with bacon drippings.

I'm an agnostic with regard to fine dining. Back in my lawyering days, I used to say if I never again set foot in a restaurant, I not only wouldn't miss it; I wouldn't realize it.

But, immersed in food at a place like Highlands, I'm capable of enjoying every moment. It's like playing golf well but despising golf as a game. Playing or not playing, eating well or not, you've got both options covered.

We ordered off the dinner menu, for me seared and braised duck on a bed of quinoa and wild rice with carrots, young turnips and Appleton Estate rum, for her grilled black grouper served over a root vegetable puree with black truffle and mushroom relish.

We ate without many words, the room's conversational drone providing background, nothing but an occasional exclamation from us at the surprising flavors.

And after the eating and drinking, too sated for dessert, there was finally nothing left to do but the leaving.

So we walked out of the restaurant in a tentative sort of way, awkward, pausing outside the door on the sidewalk, looking across the little plaza at Highlands United Methodist Church, its mission-style clay tile roof rising incongruously above Birmingham's Five Points South.

After a few moments, Sally leaned into me, grasped my upper arm, looked up and said: "I'm not ready to be alone yet tonight. Wait for the valet to bring my car, then follow me to my place. It's not far. We can talk there."

I followed the coach's Skate to a ten-story condominium on Birmingham's Southside in a neighborhood near Highland Park. A gate on the ground floor admitted her to the underground parking deck; I parked on the street and met her in the lobby.

Sally Kronenberg lived on the tenth floor of the building. On the entire tenth floor, I learned, when the elevator opened inside her apartment.

Lightly varnished blond floors, Scandinavian furniture, large-scale contemporary art. Miele coffeemaker, Bosch and Woolf appliances. "You are a woman full of surprises, Sally Kronenberg," I said.

She reached behind her, and the silk dress puddled at her feet. "Surprise!" she said.

I reached to cup the small of her back with one hand. "That was no surprise," I said and kissed her.

CHAPTER EIGHTEEN

Saturday January 28

When I woke up, I was alone. I found my boxers on the other side of the nightstand and found Sally in the living room sitting with one leg tucked under her in the Morris chair in front of the big windows. She was drinking something out of a steaming mug, and the room smelled of fresh coffee.

"Hey," I said.

She looked up. "Hey yourself. I thought you were going to sleep through the weekend."

"Hmm. Coffee smells good. What's for breakfast?

"Coffee is around the corner in the kitchen. There's a mug for you above the coffeemaker. But I have to warn you; I'm no cook."

"That's fine. If there's bread, I'll make toast, if there's a toaster."

"There's bread and a toaster. There's even orange marmalade and yogurt and strawberries if you want that. I said I don't cook, not that I don't eat."

I started on a mug of coffee while I toasted two slices of bread, smeared marmalade on them, sliced three strawberries into a bowl, and covered them with vanilla yogurt. I placed the food on a tray and carried it into the living room while Sally sipped her coffee. We sat that way for a few minutes before I asked Sally a question that had floated into my head as I awoke.

"Why did you say 'them'?"

"What?"

"Back there in Akilah's room. You said 'We have to get them.' Why 'them'? Why 'we'?"

Sally sipped her coffee and stared out the window so long I decided she must not have heard me. Finally, she looked back at me. "I suppose I should tell you. I knew Don Kramer pretty well."

"So you knew what he worked on?"

She nodded. "About three years ago, when Kris was a sophomore, I attended three of her high school soccer games and a few practices. Kris was not the reason I first began to attend games there. I was recruiting a couple of senior girls on the team who ended up playing soccer at North Carolina. We have a good program at Southern, but I can't compete with an ACC school."

She was silent for a moment, sipping her coffee. Having little to say myself, I raised a palm in a half-shrug.

"So. Don was always very involved in Kris's soccer. He would help prepare the practice field, cut the grass, mark lines. I guess he was a soccer dad.

"Of course, I began to see that Kris had potential, and I made it a policy to talk to all the parents anyway. Don and I would stand on the sideline and talk soccer and women's sports. Then one day after practice, he asked me if I'd like to get coffee at a little place he'd discovered in the Lakefront District."

She looked out the window again. This time I knew not to speak. After a while, she said, "Don and I became lovers that afternoon."

Into my silence, Sally said, "You're not saying anything."

"You noticed," I said.

"I did. Notice. Are you all right?"

I drank some coffee. "I'm fine. Might be better if this coffee had a little bourbon mixed in, but I'm okay."

She swung around to look at me. "I do hope so. I'm not a teen-ager nor a Mormon nor a Baptist. Not that being one of those would stop anyone from having a sex life." She reached out to touch my hand, still holding the coffee mug. "Listen, I'm not perfect. I'm flawed. I'm a woman. I like men."

"I'm pretty sure neither of those conditions qualifies as a flaw."

Almost a chuckle. "I hope you're right." She shrugged. "I liked Don Kramer. Cared about him. And I like you."

"So you brought Kramer here. . . ."

"Off and on until about six months ago." "Oh," she said. "Not *here* here. Not then. Another place closer to campus. I moved to this building about fifteen months ago. Don didn't want me in that part of town anymore."

She touched my hand again. "Oh," she said.

"You say that often."

"Hmmph. No I don't. Just when I'm explaining an old relationship to someone new. I meant to say, Oh, if you were thinking, Don and I had a one-night stand, or a 'fling,' no, it wasn't like that. That's not my style. And it wasn't his. No. We were together almost three years. I miss him. He, uhh, he broke off with me about six months ago. He said he wanted to try to make his family closer. I haven't been around him, really, since then. Still. I'm going to miss him for a long time."

Into my silence, she said, "Maybe I should have told you last night. But I didn't want last night to get complicated or . . . truncated. That was hardly a time for a history lesson. And after all, I didn't ask you to describe your entire past." She took the mug from me, placed it on the floor, and this time took my hand. "What can I say? I don't want this to be a problem for us. Please tell me it won't."

Kramer was a good man. I knew this for a fact. Sally's relationship with him would cost me nothing. I told her so. We did not speak of it again.

After breakfast Sally and I spent another hour or so deepening our acquaintance. After which, I faced one of life's existential decisions:

shower now, put on yesterday's clothes and change at the hotel, or wait to shower after returning to the hotel. I opted for a modification. Shower now, dress commando-style in yesterday's clothes, drive back to the Tutwiler, and change there.

The police department's daily press conference on Kris Kramer's disappearance had been aired by a local television station every day since the day after Kris disappeared. I hadn't watched. Inane questions, stock responses. Unfortunately, although Sally knew a few facts about the cases Kramer worked on, she said she knew nothing of a New Orleans connection and that she had never heard Kramer mention a client or a witness named Godchaux. In short, Sally knew less then I knew, and that wasn't much. I was back at the hotel alone, there was a television in the hotel room and it was time for the press conference, so before changing clothes, I turned on the TV and sat down to watch on the lumpy swivel chair near the window.

Leon Grubbs stood ramrod straight behind a lectern, looking like an actor playing a police captain, his perfectly-shaven face appearing almost blue under the lights. As Grubbs began to read a statement, my cell phone rang. I hit the mute button on the remote.

It was Leon Grubbs. "Slate," he said.

"I'm pretty busy now, Captain. Watching your media performance. I'm guessing it was taped."

"7:00 sharp this morning, every morning. I think I look my best early, don't you?"

"Always good to make the best of a bad situation."

"Yeah. Thanks. Look, Slate, I wanted to let you know something before you heard it through the media or somewhere else. My colleagues in the white coats down in forensics tell me Kramer wasn't killed down at the tracks. The body was moved there and dumped. Just thought you should know."

I watched Grubbs' image on the television screen mouthing silent syllables into the microphones.

"Slate, you there?"

"Still here. Watching you speak without sound."

"What?"

"Nothing. I appreciate the call. And the information. Anything else new?"

"No sir. Any time you know something, unlikely as that seems, feel free to share."

"Will do, Captain."

"Right. See you around, Slate."

I turned off the television, undressed and hung up yesterday's coat and trousers. I fetched a towel from the bathroom, spread it over my cushion, and sat with a clear mind for ten minutes, then got up to get dressed.

I had just knotted my tie perfectly after only the second try when a man's booming voice announced: "Room service!"

Said announcement accompanied a heavy knock on the door. When I checked the peephole, I could not see a thing, though the device had worked fine when I checked in.

Like many hotel rooms, the closet in mine, with mirrored sliding doors, occupied a space adjacent to the hall door.

I slid the closet door farthest from the hall door open quietly so I could not be seen standing in the bathroom across from the closet, unlocked the hall door, and stepped just inside the bathroom.

As I expected, for about twenty seconds nothing happened. I waited with the little Ruger in my right hand, my mind still, my diaphragm moving quietly in and out.

The doorknob turned slowly, then the door burst open and a heavy figure in a black sweatshirt and jeans charged in like a fullback trying to make the first down on third and short. As he passed the bathroom door, I accommodated him with a shoulder to the midsection and a leg whip.

His head slammed into the mirrored closet door, shattering the glass and spraying fragments over both of us. Under his right hand was a nickel-plated Bulldog forty-four.

I wanted to think he'd lost his grip on the stubby gun from my ferocious assault, but his sudden loss of strength could have been the result of the six-inch shard of glass protruding from the back of his hand.

I kicked the gun away and put a knee hard into his left kidney. The kick sent the gun skittering across the floor and dislodged the glass. The back of his hand began to spurt blood.

Since he wasn't holding a gun anymore, I showed him mine by sticking the barrel in his right eye. "Room service? Didn't anyone tell you I'm a lousy tipper?"

He grunted but did not move. "Don't get up," I said.

I stood up and pointed the Ruger at him, pulled my cell phone out of my jacket pocket, and dialed 911.

In five minutes or so, the room filled with cops, if you can call "filling" the sudden presence of two uniforms who must have been in the neighborhood eating doughnuts and drinking coffee.

It seemed longer, but I didn't really count, since I didn't often look at my watch, obliged as I was to keep pointing the gun at my guest, and his snappy repartee, consisting of variations of grunts and shakes of the head, caused time to creep by in its petty pace.

"What's going on here?"

The bigger and older of the two cops, a black man with graying hair, thick arms and shoulders, and a belly that his service belt didn't hide anymore, pointed his Glock at me and told me to put my gun down.

The other cop, younger, with crewcut blond hair and an angular face, had come in behind and to one side and pointed his gun at Mr. Room Service.

I tossed the little .380 on the bed and told them my name and described what had happened. "And, for what it's worth, Captain Grubbs bought me a cup of coffee last week."

"You know Captain Grubbs?" the younger cop said. "Leon Grubbs?"

"That's the one," I said.

"Just a minute," he said. He spoke into his radio, and we all listened to the static; then my cell phone rang.

"Slate? Grubbs. I don't want to talk to you. Hand the phone to the officer."

The younger officer identified himself and listened for thirty seconds. "All right, sir," he said and tossed the phone back to me. "We're going to take this guy down to the station and book him for B&E and assault."

The older cop holstered his gun, pulled on a pair of latex gloves, and snapped handcuffs on the man on the floor. He looked up at me.

"Make yourself useful, Slate. Give me a hand towel so this guy doesn't bleed all over this fine hotel."

The cop took the hand towel and tied it expertly around the bleeding hand. He got Mr. Room Service to his feet and headed out the door.

The younger cop started to follow, but at the door stopped, turned back and said, "Oh, yeah, Grubbs said to tell you to call him in an hour. And he told me one other thing."

"What's that, officer?" I asked.

"Please leave Birmingham and never come back."

He said it with a smirk. I was in no position to take offense.

CHAPTER NINETEEN

I checked out of the Tutwiler after retrieving the notes and the memory stick from the safe in the hotel basement and drove the Taurus three blocks to the parking deck behind the Sheraton next to Birmingham's Civic Center, just north of I-20.

All the way up at the top of the deck, you drive out onto the top floor and suddenly feel like you're outside again, the only roof the sky.

Today the roof-sky was a leaden gray, producing a cold mist unworthy of windshield wipers. So much for upbeat weather forecasts.

I backed into a parking space, the rear bumper only a few inches from an eight-story drop to the street below. Here, I had a view of the entrance to the top floor of the deck.

I locked the doors and pulled the Glock out of the holster and placed it on the seat. If Matt Damon were playing me in a movie, this would be the place where the obligatory chase scene began, the hero's and villain's cars careening around the parking deck smashing into civilians' rides, bullets flying, fake tire squeals filling the theater.

But this was real life, and the only person I saw for fifteen minutes was an old man with a scruffy fringe of white hair who drove his dirty red Toyota pickup around the deck twice before he found the exit.

By then it seemed no new grunters had followed me from the Tutwiler, and I got out, locked the door, retrieved my bags from the trunk, and rode the parking deck elevator down to the lobby. I paid in cash for one night and showed the Pakistani clerk a driver's license issued by New Mexico that said my name was Wallace George.

He gave me the card key after the usual spiel about a morning paper and how to find the hotel restaurant. Birmingham isn't such a hotbed for conventions, believe it or not, and the hotel didn't exactly seem overbooked.

I declined the offer of a bellman and found the room after an elevator ride and a quarter-mile hike. The side of my hand was a little sore, but that was nothing compared to the damage I would have done to myself if I had used my knuckles on my unexpected guest. I took the ice bucket out, found the ice machine, filled the bucket, then made an ice pack for my hand with the plastic bucket liner. I sat at the desk chair looking out the window at the view of industrial plants, and, in the middle distance, the airport. Now I knew two things I had not known yesterday. Someone wanted to know something badly enough – information they thought I possessed – to send that amateur to my hotel room. They might send a pro next time. And if anyone knew of the relationship between Kramer and Sally. . . .

I picked up my cell phone and keyed in Sally's office number. No answer, so I tried her cell. No answer there either. I left a voice mail asking her to call.

I was just about to head back to the law firm when the hotel phone rang. I lifted the receiver and answered.

"Slate," said a voice. "Leon Grubbs." Grubbs somehow managed in three syllables to convey both resignation and exasperation.

"Hello, Chief."

"Deputy Chief Grubbs, Sir, to you. For some reason, Slate, I keep having to intervene to keep you out of the lockup. Believe it or not, I'm actually becoming a little tired of it. So, next time, if there is a next time, and there won't be, I may not recognize your name, if you understand me."

"Understood. But how did you find me here?"

"I'm a trained detective. Slate, I have a couple of people with me who want to talk to you. I can't imagine why. Although I have better things to do than visit your hotel room, it's better that we come up there. Comprende?"

"I was just leaving. Can't you bring them to Woolf White?"

"No, I can't. We're here now, and we're coming up. You stay put. But, there is another thing."

"What's that?"

"Like every crime victim, you have the right to know the identity of your – uhh – assailant. Guy's name is Billy Royal. Walker County peckerwood. No major priors; assault, petty theft, drunk and disorderly."

"Known to work for anyone in particular?"

"Not really. Funny though. DA's office says he's already hired a lawyer. May not stay in our jail very long. Anyway. We're on the way up."

Thirty seconds later Grubbs knocked on the door. With him were agents Sanders and Alston.

Grubbs turned to the two FBI agents. "So here he is in all his glory. Agents Sanders and Alston, Mr. Slate. Slate, Agents Sanders and Alston."

"We've met. . . ." Agent Sanders began, but Grubbs did not seem to hear.

"I hope the three of you have fun, Grubbs said. I have some police work to do." He was on his way to the door before I could speak, but he stopped with the door open. "And, Slate?"

"Yes, sir, Detective Grubbs?"

He held the door for a moment, then shook his head. "Never mind. Call me." And he walked out, the door closing with a thump behind him.

I shook hands with the two FBI agents, and they sat on the side of the bed. I sat in the desk chair.

"I see that you wore the WalMart shoes today, agent Alston. Just for me?"

Alston left his gaze steady on me. "No, I upgraded today. Usually wear the WalMart cap toes. But these are the Costco wingtips. My aunt bought me a membership."

Maybe Alston scored higher on IQ tests than his shoe size after all. "So how did Grubbs – Detective Grubbs – find me here? I did not give the hotel my real name, you know."

They looked at each other, and Agent Sanders spoke.

"Detective Grubbs didn't find you here. He just agreed to accompany us after we spoke to him first thing this morning. You'd be surprised what an FBI badge and a recent photograph will do for the memory of a hotel desk clerk."

"I see." I'd have to remember that when I spoke to Grubbs. I looked at Agent Sanders with a sudden flash of understanding. "So, did you two trash my boat?"

"Mr. Slate, if we had wanted to search your boat, we would have shown up at the dock with a search warrant."

"Sure you would. Unless you didn't."

"And if we had conducted such an unlawful search, sir, not that we would have, sir, you would never have known we were there, sir."

"So to make it look like it wasn't you guys, you searched my boat and trashed it."

Agent Alston spoke up. "You two are making my head hurt. You know we fibbies aren't that smart, Slate."

Agent Sanders nodded. "Look, Slate, we need to work together. The FBI doesn't usually investigate murders, but we don't ignore them either. I personally feel a sense of urgency after this last one. We both need the information on that memory stick, but you don't have the resources to retrieve it. I do."

"Memory stick?"

Sanders rolled her eyes. "We do investigate, you know."

"But how did you know about the memory stick?"

"Your friend Moeller seems to enjoy a drink with a friendly FBI agent."

"I see." Herr Moeller. "Well played, Ms. Sanders. But I usually work alone."

"On this one you need our help, and besides, we were on this before you were, and you know the bureau is the first level of law enforcement in any kidnapping case."

"Sure, but what exactly are you talking about?"

Agent Sanders speared me with those unmatched eyes and said, "We think you know, but in any case, we are here to deliver an invitation."

"I'm invited to an event? A dinner party? A soirée? I don't believe I've ever had an invitation from an FBI agent before."

She shook her head. "The United States attorney would like you to come down to the federal building – with us – and talk with her about this matter that it seems, whether we like it or not, we're both working on."

"You know you work for an unconstitutional agency."

"Maybe so," said Alston, "but we're hell at solving encryption algorithms."

"Well. I suppose you are, at that." I stood, walked to the window and looked out. In the distance I could see Legion Field, where Paul Bryant had leaned, so effortless and casual, so many years ago, against a goal post, a real-life John Wayne in a houndstooth hat.

A little farther south, on a hill overlooking old steel mill neighborhoods, sprawled the Alabama Southern campus, where I'd found the body of an innocent young girl.

I turned back toward the room and Mr. and Ms. FBI. "All right," I said. "I'll meet with you and the U.S. attorney."

"Good," said Agent Sanders. "See?" she said to Agent Alston. "I told you he'd come around."

"Did I have a choice?" I asked.

"No," Alston said.

"When is this meeting proposed?" I said.

"Now," Sanders answered.

"The government at work on a Saturday?"

"You'd be surprised," Sanders said.

"I'll get my coat and hat," I said.

CHAPTER TWENTY

Tweedledee and Tweedledum, uhh, that is, Agents Sanders and Alston, escorted me out of the hotel, and we walked shoulder to shoulder up Richard Arrington Boulevard and underneath I-20.

I felt like explaining to other pedestrians that this was not a perp walk, but I doubted that my escorts would appreciate the humor.

Agent Sanders held a cell phone to her ear with one hand and hoisted an umbrella against the cold mist with the other. Alston trudged along beside me, occasionally bumping into my shoulder, no doubt to assert his jurisdiction.

Our ten-minute walk took us past the Birmingham Museum of Art, the Jefferson County Courthouse, the Tutwiler hotel, and the headquarters buildings of Birmingham's major banks and law firms.

On the damp streets, a few men and women, most in some kind of rain gear, walked quickly, coats and umbrellas held close, eyes squinting against the wind and rain.

As we passed the front doors of One Federal Place, a modern eleven-story building of gray granite and blue-tinted glass, Alston held up one hand and spoke into my ear. "Let's duck in here for a second," he said.

"What's going on?" I said. I nodded at the blue-tinted windows of the building's lobby restaurant. "You have a sudden craving for chicken salad?"

"Lay off the smart comments for once, Slate. I'm trying to do you a favor."

Alston turned to his partner. "Go ahead to the offices and get the lawyers ready," he said. "We'll be right behind you."

Sanders nodded and walked on past the fountain in the building's plaza and toward the federal reserve branch bank on the corner.

I followed Alston into the building. "Come on, Slate," he said. You're going to thank me for this."

He walked past the elevator entrance at the rear of the large lobby.

Behind the elevators, a smaller alcove partially concealed the doors to the lobby restrooms. In front of the men's room sat a cleaning cart with a yellow "Temporarily Closed" banner.

Alston sidestepped the cart and pushed the frosted glass door completely open.

Inside, an attendant wearing iPod headphones swabbed one of the stalls. I hung back with no idea why we were here.

Alston tapped the attendant on the elbow and held out his FBI identification wallet. "We need privacy for a few minutes, friend," he said. "Take a break." The attendant nodded, said something that might have been "Yep," and disappeared out the door.

Alston moved the cart inside and closed the door so the cart blocked the door from anyone trying to enter.

"All right, sport," he said. "You're carrying two items that you don't want to be carrying when we see the marshals at the U.S. attorney's building. One inside the jacket, one on the ankle."

"You're good," I said.

"I can be even better," Alston said. "You can just hand me the items. I'm not going to take them off you. I'll carry them through the metal detector and keep them on me till you leave the building. The marshals know I'm carrying so they won't say a word to me. But since you're a lawyer, I'm sure you know it's a federal offense to show up at the door of a federal facility with a weapon. The marshals might look the other way since you're with me, but what's the point in making them decide? And even if they did, they won't hold them for you, and I will."

I couldn't argue with his logic, and I had no doubt that Alston would return the guns to me as he promised. Otherwise, I could complain to his partner, Strangeeyes. Or the U.S. attorney. Or the president. He surely wouldn't cling to my guns.

I handed over the guns. He stuck the Glock in his jacket pocket, strapped the Ruger on his ankle, nodded, and we walked out.

The office of the United States attorney for the Northern District of Alabama resides in a nondescript, or, more precisely, ugly brown brick building on Fourth Avenue North, diagonally across Eighteenth Street from the Hugo L. Black federal courthouse, named for the state's only United States Supreme Court justice.

From outside, the building housing the offices of the U.S. attorney might be mistaken for a document depository or an unsold renovation. Closer inspection revealed the inevitable presence of the metal detector and X-ray machines just a few feet inside the entrance, staffed by a phalanx of United States marshals, if a couple of aging and none-too-fit gentlemen perching on what looked like cheap bar stools amounted to a phalanx.

The present United States attorney for the Northern District, Katherine Parker, was the third female U.S. attorney in a row for the district. Back in 2000, George W. appointed a former state court judge to the post. The former judge's husband, a wealthy businessman, had donated bushels of money to the Republican party.

Barack Obama appointed a long-serving assistant United States attorney to the job. Her grandfather had served for two terms as chief justice of the Alabama Supreme Court. An uncle serving on the Fifth Circuit Court of Appeals had died in 1989 when he attempted to disarm a man who walked just in front of him thorough a revolving door into the courthouse lobby in Houston, pulled out a gun and began firing at random. A federal marshal stepped out of the elevator, drew his weapon, and killed the lunatic with two shots.

United States Attorney Katherine Parker did not keep me waiting. When Alston and I reached Parker's outer office, Sanders was seated on a black tufted leather couch against a wall opposite a secretary's desk. Otherwise, the room was empty.

Sanders looked up at us.

"They're ready," she said.

At the same moment, the door to the inner office opened. A pretty young black woman, her hair held in back by some sort of leather and dowel contraption, came through and closed the door behind her.

"Good morning, Agent Alston," she said.

"Good morning, Molly," Alston said. Molly glanced at me. "This is Mr. Slate," Alston told her. He made it sound like an apology.

"So I expected," said Molly. She nodded at me. "Mr. Slate."

"Molly," I said.

"I apologize, Mr. Slate. I am Molly Blevins, U.S. Attorney Parker's legal assistant. Ms. Parker and the others are ready to see you now." She opened the inner office door and gestured with her other hand for us to enter.

Katherine Parker had arranged her office much like a number of judges I knew arranged theirs. Her desk sat on the diagonal in a corner of the room. Perpendicular to the desk were two conference tables arranged end-to-end to create one conference table around twelve feet in length.

The walls were covered with bookshelves and prints of famous lawyers and presidents and a green felt wallpaper that would not have been out of place in a men's club in London.

Around the table sat three young assistant United States attorneys, and, seated at her desk, the United States attorney herself.

Parker stood after we had entered the room and Molly Blevins had closed the door. Agents Sanders and Alston took seats at the table on my right. Parker wore a dark gray suit over a red silk blouse with vertical tuxedo pleats. She held gold-rimmed reading glasses in her left hand and wore minimal makeup.

"Mr. Slate, my name is Katherine Parker," she said. "I am the United States attorney in this district. Thank you for coming in for this meeting."

I nodded. "Thank you for the. . . ." I glanced at Alston. "The invitation."

"Please understand, Mr. Slate, that the leaders of my task force on this case were prepared to meet with you whenever you were ready. This office has committed substantial resources to this case, and your involvement represents a significant development. I hope Agent Sanders and Agent Alston made that clear."

She looked at Sanders, who raised her eyebrows slightly. "Well," Parker said, sitting down. "Let's get started. Mr. Clark?"

One of the attorneys on my left sat forward.

"Mr. Slate, Thomas Clark. The former U.S. attorney in this office appointed me to head this district's task force on corruption in government. Ms. Parker kept me in that position. The task force. . . ."

"Stop," I said. "Task force? Government corruption?"

Clark nodded. "Yes. The task force was formed five years ago. . . ."

"Wait," I held out a hand. "I appreciate that you have a presentation to make, Mr. Clark. But I didn't sign on to any task force on government corruption. I'm not in politics, and I'm not interested in taking scalps from politicians. I'm just a simple guy who tries to help clients with problems. I was hired to find a missing girl. That's all."

Katherine Parker spoke. "We understand and appreciate your position, Mr. Slate. All of us here, well, except Ms. Sanders, are lawyers. Ms. Sanders' background, as you may know, is in forensic accounting. I'm sure we would all someday like to return to basics and lead uncomplicated lives. But when a person chooses to practice law or accounting, he or she leaves simplicity behind. I think you need to hear us out. I think you would show us that professional courtesy. Your reputation indicates that your behavior towards other professionals, other lawyers, has always been more respectful than your rhetoric. In any event, we can help each other here."

"I behave in a more civil manner than I talk. Some might say it's the other way around. But, all right, Ms. Parker, you win. This time. I'm here. Might as well listen. I might learn something." I thought of Don Kramer's comment to me about knowing how to listen.

"Indeed you might, as we may as well. Mr. Clark?"

"Yes, thanks. Well, as I was saying, Mr. Slate, five years ago, Ms. Parker's predecessor formed a task force on corruption in Alabama state government. Initially, that task force focused on corruption in the two-year college system, and its work led to indictments and prosecutions. After we discovered the connections among the persons of interest and defendants in that investigation and gambling interests, the office of the U.S. attorney for the Middle District of Alabama launched an investigation into the influence of gambling money in state government. As you know, that investigation also led to indictments of gambling kingpins, lobbyists, and legislators. Even a few confessions and pleas of guilty."

"And several not guilty verdicts."

"Yes. But information turned up by that task force caused us here in this district to regroup our two-year college task force and start a new investigation into inroads made by elements of organized crime into state government."

Clark paused to take a sip of water.

"And then our investigation took an unexpected turn."

He looked up from his notes and looked down the table at me. "You know where I'm headed now, don't you?"

"The oil and gas business," I said.

"You got it. Nearly everyone in Alabama has heard of the Exxon case. The State of Alabama sued Exxon for breach of contract because, it alleged, Exxon charged unrelated costs against Alabama's share and cheated the state out of royalty payments. The Cunningham, Bounds firm out of Mobile represented the state and won a multi-billion dollar verdict."

"Most of the damages award was reversed on appeal," I said.

Clark nodded and sipped more water.

"Yes." He shrugged. "And that case had no relation to organized crime. But that is not our interest here. After the BP oil spill in the Gulf, the entire oil and gas industry viewed itself as having a target on its back. And maybe it did. Also not our interest." He raised a palm. "Not our present interest."

I said, "So, let's get to it. What is your present interest, and what does any of this have to do with finding Kris Kramer?"

Katherine Parker answered the question. "Mr. Slate, this is confidential and off the record. Do I have your agreement on that?"

I nodded.

"We believe you may have in your possession information which would assist the United States in its investigation of corruption in government related to possible bribery of state officials in Alabama and other Southern states by entities in the oil and gas business. And yes, we think it may be related to Ms. Kramer's disappearance. As you know, these FBI agents and others are working night and day on that case as well."

"The memory stick," Alston said.

"And possibly more," Parker added.

"Have you convened a grand jury?" I asked.

"That is not only confidential, but secret, but for purposes of discussion in this room only, you may assume that we have convened or will soon convene a grand jury on this case," said Parker.

"Then why didn't you just issue a subpoena to Woolf White?"

Clark answered. "We would have gotten there. We – ahh – we had information that Kramer was working on the case from the civil side. Nevertheless, the firm had not filed a lawsuit. And we knew we would face a barrage of objections on grounds of various privileges. Then Kris Kramer disappeared, and her father was killed."

"And then you showed up," Parker said.

"A stranger rides into town," Agent Sanders said quietly enough so that only my end of the table heard.

Clark continued. "There was always, also, the possibility that if Kramer and Woolf White did file a lawsuit, it would be a *qui tam* action, so we would be working together on the civil suit anyway."

"And you could use the civil suit for discovery in the criminal case," I said.

Clark nodded. "Well, maybe. There would have been limitations on that, but this office would not mind having both matters open."

"So now we all have a problem," I told them.

"Without problems, lawyers would be out of work," Clark said. "You want to tell us about a new one?"

I explained my new of counsel relationship with Woolf White and that asking me for information amounted to asking Bill Woolf for the same information. The table sat silent for what seemed like five minutes but was probably fifteen seconds.

"Well, I guess we do, at that," Parker said.

"Thanks for the invitation," I said. "It's been enlightening. But at this point, I think we should all go somewhere else and do what we have to do. Your jobs are to prosecute criminals. I am not interested in trying to eliminate government corruption, noble though that pursuit may be. I am a simple person. My job is to find Kris Kramer. And from that I shall not waver."

I stood and turned toward the door.

"Goodbye, Mr. Slate. For now," Parker said.

I nodded without turning around, opened the door, and closed it behind me.

As I left the reception area after bidding goodbye to Molly Blevins, Agent Alston caught up to me.

"Slate," he said. He gestured toward a small conference room across from Katherine Parker's office suite. "Step in here. I'm holding some property of yours."

We went into the conference room. Alston closed the door and handed my Glock back to me, then unstrapped the Ruger from his ankle and returned the small gun to me as well.

"No metal detectors on the way out," he said. "I could have handed you these outside, but Agent Sanders and I know your background. Take care, Slate."

"I appreciate your confidence," I said.

"Think about cooperating with us, Slate. Take the short way through this time instead of the long way around. You want to find a missing girl. So do we, and we want to finish this investigation."

"I'll consider it," I said.

"Do that," he said.

No one searched me on my way out. I may have been the only ordinary citizen carrying two guns in a U.S. government facility anywhere on the planet.

The marshals nodded politely as I walked through the turnstile exit.

CHAPTER TWENTY-ONE

I'd been spinning my wheels. I needed to return to basics.

I'd been hired to find a missing girl. Her father had been working up a case that could send major political players and maybe even a few career criminals – calling them mobsters was so twentieth century – to prison. I'd received a note from someone who wanted me to "STAY OUT OF THE OIL & GAS BUSNESS." Everyone, including me, seemed to think these facts were connected. I needed to find out whether they were.

Returning to basics meant talking to the right people, maybe shaking someone's cage, making something happen. Doing something even if it's wrong, and letting the rough end drag.

The employees of the federal government in that meeting wanted to find Kris Kramer no more and no less than they wanted to drink their dry martinis and eat their shrimp cocktails that night.

But the AUSAs in the Northern District of Alabama lived and died for prosecuting corrupt Alabama politicians. That was where they made their bones. And got their names in the newspapers and the political blogs. They could and would do nothing for me aside from possibly having their technicians in Washington decipher the information on the thumb drive Akilah Ziyenga had entrusted to me. Corrupt politicians were not my gig. In Alabama, maybe everywhere, crooks in government were part of the background noise.

Slogging back through the cold mist, heading toward the Sheraton, I checked my voice mail and saw that Sally had called. I hit reply without listening to the message. This time she answered.

"Hi. Where are you?" I asked.

"In my office. The girls and I sort of want to hang around together right now. Where are you?"

"Walking the streets of Birmingham in the cold rain." I told her about the incident at the Tutwiler and checking into the Sheraton and meeting with the U.S. attorney and her supporting cast. Then I said, "Look, I'm a little concerned about your safety. I'm going to ask my police contacts to increase patrols near your condo. I may have to go on a short trip."

"You know I can take care of myself. But if it makes you feel better, go ahead. Maybe it will make me feel better too."

"Good. I will make the call, and I will call you back later this afternoon."

I called Grubbs' office. He was out, but when I left the message about patrols with his administrative assistant, she promised that she would see that Grubbs gave the order.

Back at the hotel, I logged into the wireless network with the Mac and searched for Michael Godchaux in New Orleans.

There were four, none with the telephone number in Kramer's file. One Michael Godchaux, a guy I probably wouldn't mind drinking a Dixie beer with, ran public relations for the Saints. After the allegations that Saints defensive players earned bounties for injuries to opposing quarterbacks and the sanctions against Saints coaches and front-office personnel, this fellow must have felt like a long-tailed cat in a room full of rocking chairs.

Another was a senior biology major at Tulane.

A third practiced tax law with one of the oldest law firms in Louisiana. This one might be Kramer's man, but a white shoe tax law practice, even in Louisiana, most likely did not put this fellow into intimate contact with the New Orleans Mob.

The fourth Michael Godchaux had earned a degree in accounting at LSU, but I could find no information on this accountant Godchaux after he'd finished undergraduate school. That absence of information did not seem normal. Instinct told me this accountant Godchaux and the Godchaux in Kramer's notes were the same man.

I picked up my iPhone and keyed in the number for Michael Godchaux I'd memorized from Kramer's notes.

Before I called, I considered turning off the Show My Caller ID feature but decided that Godchaux would be more likely to speak with me if I left it on.

Of course, no one answered; a default canned voice mail announcement played after six rings.

I left a message asking the caller to contact me at the Woolf White law firm in Birmingham – I worked there, didn't I? – and hung up.

Ten seconds later, the iPhone rang and told me that the caller's identity was blocked. When I answered, a man's voice said "Did you call me, Mr. Slate?"

"Yes," I said. "Are you Michael Godchaux?"

"You must know that, since you called me on this phone, but yes, I am Michael Godchaux."

"I could have keyed in the wrong number."

"Yes, but you didn't. I've been expecting you to call."

"Then my hunch was right."

"What hunch?"

"You aren't the Michael Godchaux with the Saints, Michael Godchaux the tax lawyer, or Michael Godchaux the Tulane student. You are the Michael Godchaux who graduated *cum laude* from LSU in two double O two and then dropped out of sight. Am I right?"

"Hmm," Godchaux said. "I don't know. I don't believe I am completely invisible. People do step aside when I exit an elevator. The doormen in the Quarter still try to entice me inside to see the girls. But I did go to LSU, I do have an accounting degree, and my previous employer did ask me to make sure I did not Google well."

"Where are you working now?"

"I'm not. Look, I do want to speak with you, but further conversation needs to happen in person. How soon can you be in Louisiana?"

I was tempted to say, about forty minutes, but Godchaux did not seem in a mood for explanations. "How about tomorrow morning?" I suggested.

"All right," he said. "When you get here, call this number again. I'll give you instructions on meeting me somewhere downtown or in the Quarter. Don't call me again until you're south of Lake Pontchartrain."

The connection went dead.

I called Sally and told her I'd be getting an early start in the morning for the flight to New Orleans and that I'd see her when I returned tomorrow afternoon.

Then I called Bill Woolf and told him about the conversation with Godchaux. He listened without comment and told me to take care and to remember to take a pocket tape recorder with me to New Orleans. I checked the aviation weather on the Mac before shutting it down.

CHAPTER TWENTY-TWO

Sunday January 29

Lakefront Airport, on the south shore of Lake Pontchartrain, offers general aviation a close gateway to downtown New Orleans without mixing into the traffic around Louis Armstrong New Orleans International Airport, which is actually in Kenner, Louisiana, west of New Orleans.

In 2001, the city of New Orleans joined a growing list of cities that discarded long-used names for their airports and changed the names to honor either an illustrious local citizen or someone of national or international renown.

New York changed Idlewild to JFK on Christmas Eve, 1963; a few presidents later, Washington, D.C., added Ronald Reagan's last name to National Airport.

The New Orleans Airport once was called Moisant, and the FAA three-letter identifier remains MSY, for Moisant Stock Yards.

John Moisant did not protest; he died in a plane crash on his farm in 1910, where the airport that once bore his name was built during World War II. Maybe someone in City Hall decided, fifty years later, that naming the city's airport for someone who died in a plane crash wasn't such a hot idea.

In the Albatros, Birmingham to New Orleans, six hours by car, takes forty minutes.

I did not file a flight plan.

At the FBO in Birmingham, I walked through the outside gate, threw a bag into the front locker, unchocked the wheels, did a quick preflight, and had the wheels turning fifteen minutes after I parked the rental car.

I called ground clearance while I taxied across the ramp.

Recon missions, whether for practice or hot missions over enemy ground, are flown low and fast, no more than five hundred feet above ground level. I'd flown the VR and IR routes over the Southeast so many times I knew every transmission antenna and every hill from Little Rock to Jacksonville and from New Orleans to the Outer Banks.

Takeoff on runway two four shot me out dead straight toward New Orleans via Tuscaloosa and Meridian.

I'm not paranoid, but the FBI, not to mention whoever hired Mr. Room Service, appeared to enjoy an active interest in my whereabouts, and I intended to remain literally under the radar as much as possible. As a general practice, I kept "location services" turned off on the iPhone. Maybe government spooks could track it through the GPS receiver anyway, but I doubted that I was quite that interesting.

The ceiling was three thousand feet overcast, and there was a chance of rain. I leveled off at five hundred feet AGL with the throttle on the stop. The turbofan behind me screamed its approval. Jets don't like slow drivers.

Wake up, groundlings.

The approach to runway one eight right at New Orleans Lakefront takes the pilot in over Lake Pontchartrain. The sight is magnificent, but the approach does not forgive the pilot who arrives too low to a runway with a displaced threshold suspended a few yards above the oily water of the lake.

I landed and taxied to the Landmark FBO. After shutdown I climbed out and pulled the soft duffel containing my suit and street shoes out of the rear seat, locked up the cabin and carried the duffel into the restroom in the pilot's lounge to change.

Maybe one of these days I'd sell the plane and start flying Southwest to save myself the trouble of changing clothes on both ends of the flight.

But then I'd have to deal with TSA. And ship my gun in the cargo hold. And let the airline and the government know I had it.

On second thought, maybe I'd just keep on with the Clark Kent meets Top Gun act.

At the FBO counter, I picked up the keys to another rental car. What would Avis do without me?

Heading southwest on I-10 toward downtown at ten, I pulled the iPhone out of my jacket pocket and called Michael Godchaux. Phoning while driving? Try communicating with air traffic control while turning to a heading and descending. I really can multitask, state legislators, thank you very much.

Godchaux asked me to meet him in thirty minutes for brunch at Begue's in the Royal Sonesta Hotel on Bourbon Street.

I started to say no, because I didn't want to drive into the Quarter, but he had already disconnected.

As I approached downtown, my phone buzzed, and I picked it up. Godchaux had texted me: Change of plan. Same time, Le Pavilion bar. Striped blue shirt.

Better for me. I hated driving in the French Quarter. Always felt like I was about to hit a pedestrian or get arrested or kissed or flashed. Or all of the above.

I parked in the deserted post office parking lot on Girod and walked the four blocks to the corner of Poydras and Carroll Street.

Downtown New Orleans was damp, cool, and disconcertingly clean. For the moment there was no rain. The few pedestrians might have been on their way to church, maybe to St. Patrick's on Camp Street. Tourists in this part of downtown were scarce. The partiers were still sleeping off the Saturday night festivities.

Le Pavillon's facade always made me think of a wedding cake lying on its side. The portico led into a lobby that might have pleased the Bourbon kings of France, or even their wives. I walked past marble columns and turned left into Le Gallery, the lobby bar.

The bar was empty except for a white-jacketed bartender who perched on a stool reading the *Times-Picayune*.

It was around ten-thirty in the morning, too early for the bar lunches, too late for the tourists' Bloody Marys. The bartender looked up reluctantly from his paper. "Something for you, sir?" he said.

"Yes," I said. "A little information."

"Yes, sir?"

"Why didn't they spell Gallery the French way when they named the bar?"

"Excuse me, sir?"

"The name of the bar. Le Gallery. Were they trying to make some transcontinental statement? It should be The Gallery or *Le Galerie*, one or the other, don't you think?"

"I wouldn't know, sir. I moved down here from Chicago for this job, and I don't speak French. Would you like a drink, sir?"

"Actually, yes, a large chicory coffee. And I'd like to sit at the table in the corner on the right. I'm waiting for someone, a guy in a blue-striped shirt. I'd like to see him before he sees me."

I placed a ten-dollar bill on the bar, walked over to the table I'd chosen, and took a chair with my back to the wall.

From there I could see the front entrance in the mirror behind the bar. A potted plant and an ornate wooden screen shielded me from the direct vision of anyone standing in the entrance.

Ten-forty came and went, and fifteen more minutes passed by. The bartender and I were the only two people in the bar except for a middle-aged couple who must have confused the bar with the concierge's desk and wandered over to ask directions to some art gallery in the French Quarter.

I was nearly ready to ask for a real drink when the bartender looked up at me from his paper and raised his chin a little.

In the mirror I could see, just inside the entry, a heavy, short man with dark red hair, wearing a blue-striped button-down shirt, khakis, and burgundy penny loafers. He looked harmless and, as far as I could tell, unarmed. I reached into my inside jacket pocket and started the microcassette tape recorder I'd retrieved from my briefcase before leaving Birmingham.

Godchaux walked up to the bar and told the bartender he expected to meet someone. The bartender nodded in my direction. "Would that be the gentleman?" he said.

Godchaux turned in my direction. "I believe it would," he told the bartender. "Double espresso, chicory, black," he added.

I stood as Godchaux walked over and shook my hand.

"Michael Godchaux," he said. "Slate, do you mind if we sit in the other corner under the TV?"

Catching the attention of the bartender, Godchaux gestured to the flat screen monitor hanging in the opposite corner of the bar.

The bartender picked up a remote and powered on the monitor, tuned to ESPN. Talking heads discussed the NBA season.

"Moderate volume, please," Godchaux said.

I followed Godchaux to a two-top almost underneath the monitor. Somehow I doubted that Le Pavilion management referred to a table for two in Le Gallery as a two-top. I would always be more Waffle House than *haute cuisine*.

Godchaux sat with his back to the wall, and I moved my chair so I could see both the bartender and the front door. The bartender brought Godchaux's espresso, and Godchaux placed a ten-dollar bill on the table.

As the bartender retreated, Godchaux looked at me through heavy glass lenses with translucent beige frames. The lens curvature made his eyes look like blue marbles swimming in milk. "So?" he began. "You found me. Now what?"

"Do you know that Don Kramer's daughter is missing?"

"I read about it online, on al.com. Kramer didn't mention it. I know nothing of Kramer personally. He's a lawyer, and I suppose I'm a client. Was a client," he corrected himself. "I do know about Kramer's death. But I didn't know he had a daughter or that his child was missing before I read it in the newspaper. Is there some connection to the *qui tam* case?"

"Yes. I think there is a connection, but I can't connect the dots. I hoped you might have information that would help. And just so you know, finding the daughter – Kris – is why I'm here. It's what I was hired to do. I really don't care what your involvement may have been with regard to the issues Kramer was investigating, except to the extent that you have knowledge that may lead to finding Kris. Understood?"

Godchaux nodded, the eyes swimming behind the eyeglasses. "Yes," he said. "I have no idea whether I have any knowledge that will assist you at all, Mr. Slate."

"It's just Slate. I don't know whether it will help me, either. But do I infer correctly that you are willing to answer some questions?"

"Yes."

"You said you expected me to call. How did you know my name?"

Godchaux sipped his espresso. "A day or two before Kramer died, he called me from an airplane and gave me your name. Told me if anything happened to him you would eventually call me."

"So it seems that Kramer arranged this meeting. How did you and Kramer meet?"

"I called him. In the course of my work with my former employer, from time to time I acquired information I thought might someday be useful to me. Kramer's history with the Louisiana oil and gas business was part of that information."

"If Kramer wanted us to meet, don't you think he wanted you to relate to me everything you had told him?"

Godchaux glanced up at the bartender. His back was to us, and he was drying whiskey tumblers.

Godchaux's eyes swam toward me again, and he shrugged. "Everything? I don't know. But something important? Something essential? Yes. I just don't know what that essential fact might be."

"Then we need to begin at the beginning."

Godchaux shook his head. "Don't waste my time. I want to help, but I don't want to spend one second more speaking with you in public than necessary. You tell me what you know. I'll fill in the gaps."

So I told Godchaux about Kramer's visit to me, about my walk down to the railroad tracks in the middle of the night in the rain, about my meetings with Leon Grubbs and Susan Kramer, about the note on my computer, the clumsy attack in the hotel room, about the files at the Woolf firm, about the handwritten notes in the sealed file, about the memory stick, about my pleasant meeting with the feds, about Akilah Ziyenga.

I skipped the funeral, and I left out the soccer coach and the image of Kramer's unseeing eyes staring up into the cold winter rain.

When I finished, Godchaux looked at me for several seconds without speaking.

Finally, I spoke. "What did I leave out?"

"I'm sorry," Godchaux said. "I'm trying to decide what to tell you and where to begin. You know a little, but it's like you see the outside of a building without knowing anything about the interior. You know less than I expected."

"The memory stick."

Godchaux nodded. "What you don't know is really the meat of the *qui tam* case." He nodded again. "Okay. Here we go.

"You have been told and you have seen information that some Alabama public officials may have been cut in on what was essentially a skimming, or underreporting, operation conducted by oil production companies to the detriment of small lessors of oil and gas lands to these companies. And that this, should I say, revenue-sharing arrangement occurred because of the background of litigation over similar issues in Alabama, going back twenty or thirty years."

"The producers were buying protection," I said.

"Protection from lawsuits, protection from prosecution," Godchaux nodded. "But the information you have is conclusory and derivative. No proof.

"I provided the proof to Kramer. Names, deposits, bank transfers, bank account numbers."

"How?"

Godchaux sighed. "Well. Short version of the whole story. In my last semester at LSU, I encountered a little problem with a professor in a senior tax accounting class. For some reason the guy must have thought I was gay. I'm not. This professor came on to me in his office, and I rejected him. I had to reject him physically. Shoved him away and got out the door.

"I didn't tell anyone, and I figured it was over. Then, after the final exam, but before graduation, the department head summoned me to his office. This professor had accused me of cheating on the final. I did not cheat. I could have aced that exam before the semester started. It was an easy class.

"I had to tell someone. I had this uncle, my mother's brother, who worked as the business manager for a big commercial fishing outfit. My parents were dead; they died in a car crash when I was five. Various uncles and aunts took turns raising me.

"So I told my uncle about this thing with the professor. Twenty-four hours later the department head saw me walking into CEBA, the college of business building. They renamed the building a few years ago. Now it's Patrick Taylor Hall. Anyway, the accounting department head asked me again to step into his office. I figured this was it. I was being expelled.

"The department head sat down behind his desk and looked out the window. He told me to sit down, but he never looked at me. After a few seconds, he said in a very calm manner – he had this very deep, resonant voice, probably from smoking a pipe – 'A very serious mistake has been made. Your final grade in the tax course has been reinstated. Professor Downey has withdrawn any charges about academic misconduct, and all documents related to those allegations have been destroyed.'"

Godchaux sipped his espresso. "After graduation my uncle told me I should go to see a named partner in one of the big downtown law firms. I've forgotten his name, and I think he's passed on. I laughed and said, 'Uncle Ray, I'm not a lawyer.' And he said, 'The lawyer will introduce you to someone. You need to go,' and he gave me the telephone number and address.

"So I made an appointment, put on my interview suit and drove down from Baton Rouge. The lawyer turned out to be one of those half-retired guys who put on their suits every day and go to their offices just to have a place to go and read the paper and drink coffee in peace. I don't think he had an assistant; the receptionist showed me in. Great office. Top floor, great view of the city. Lots of trinkets from the oil business lying around, stock and bond announcements in Lucite – you've seen this stuff. I guess the old man was quite the oil and gas lawyer in his day. Exceedingly polite. Perfect combover. Blue seersucker suit with white bucks. Comes around the desk, shakes my hand. Then he opens an inner door and gestures. Shows me into what was obviously once his work room, not that he worked much anymore. An antique table, old, made of smooth but unstained wood. Maybe barn wood."

Godchaux shrugged. "Anyway. Sitting at the table is a guy who looks like Paul Sorvino." Godchaux raised his eyebrows. "You know the movie *Goodfellas*? That's the guy. So this guy half stands, shakes my hand, tells me to sit down. 'I understand you're a fine accounting student,' he says. Sounds like he's from Brooklyn, like some natives of New Orleans do.

"I say something self-effacing, then he says, 'So would you like to come work for me?' And I say, I don't even know what business you're in. He cocks his head a little and then he says, 'The money business.' Then he makes that apologetic palm-up gesture, you know? Mostly oil and gas properties, he says, a few other things. We need someone young, eager to learn, he says. Someone both competent and discreet. Then he names a salary that I'm sure is fifty per cent more than any other recent LSU accounting graduates are earning.

"So I took the job. That was eleven years ago."

"But you are no longer employed there, I assume," I said.

"Correct."

"You take some precautions. But you don't mind walking around New Orleans during the day. Are you sure that's safe?"

"The Michael they know has dark hair, doesn't wear glasses, dresses well, and is thirty pounds lighter. Hey," he said, "If De Niro could gain sixty pounds to play Jake LaMotta, I figure I can do thirty to stay alive."

"If this becomes a federal criminal matter, you could end up in the witness protection program."

Godchaux shook his head. "I don't think so. If I learned – or taught myself – anything in those eleven years, it's how to disappear." He patted his jacket pocket. "Second passport. Different name."

When I didn't respond, Godchaux went on. "Right. So, you need to know whether I can help you find Kris Kramer. Sorry. I have no idea where she is."

"The memory stick."

Godchaux nodded slowly. "Amazing how the capacity of those little thumb drives has grown in just a few years. Have you spoken with anyone else about it?"

I went over Moeller's efforts without using his name and explained in a general way that the United States attorney's office had expressed interest in the data on the memory stick. Godchaux listened without comment.

"Have the feds offered you anything in exchange for the data?" Godchaux asked when I had finished.

I had decided what I wanted from the feds, but I wasn't about to share that with Godchaux. "Not exactly. More on the order of you give us the stick, we do the decryption and share the data with you. And in the interim allow you the pleasure of working with a real live U.S. government agency."

Godchaux cleared his throat and leaned forward slightly. "I trust you, Slate, so here goes. He lowered his voice a couple of decibels. "I created the file on the memory stick, Slate. And I can give you the password. I could give you the decryption key as well, but why not let the government have their fun? It's not unbreakable. And you should get something out of their desire for those data. So I'd suggest you extract some exchange from the government in addition to their agreeing to decrypt the information on that thumb drive. At the very least, it will give you more time while they work on the data."

"Why don't you just tell me what's there?"

Godchaux sighed. "It's pages and pages of data. Real pump volumes and reported ones. Information about payments and payoffs. It's all there. Everything you need. I don't have the details. That's why you create the document."

I nodded. "I think I know what the government will give me in exchange. But surely Kramer wasn't ready to file a lawsuit based on the notes I saw in his file. Did you give him any other information?"

"Yeah, I did. But I don't believe any of that information would assist you in finding Kris Kramer."

Godchaux went up to the bar and borrowed a pen, then returned to the table and unfolded a cocktail napkin to one sheet. He wrote the password, an email address and a telephone number on the thin paper.

"Here," he said. "I've communicated past my comfort zone with the telephone number you used to contact me. This one is untraceable. So is the email address. Memorize."

The password and the telephone number were easy; the Hushmail email address, random numbers at Hushmail.com, not so easy. I looked at the information for a few moments, the rhythm of the numbers playing through my head like a melody. "Okay," I said.

Godchaux tore off the square of the napkin containing the numbers, produced a cigarette lighter, and before the bartender knew it had happened, the paper had turned to smoke and ash.

CHAPTER TWENTY-THREE

Back at Lakefront Airport, I called Bill Woolf on his cell and told him I needed to see him at his office first thing in the morning. He did not seem all that pleased to hear from me on Sunday morning, but he promised to meet me at seven-thirty in his office the next day.

On the other hand, Sally seemed quite pleased to hear from me. I sent her a text and caught her shopping at Whole Foods. "Sunday morning is the best time to do anything in Alabama except any time when an Alabama football game is on TV," she texted back. "All the Baptists are in church. Both times? LOL!" I told her I would connect with her when I landed in Birmingham.

In the FBO to check the aviation weather, I reflected on my conversation with Michael Godchaux and the questions it raised.

By nature, I'm a skeptic.

A few years after the first Gulf War ended, a lawyer in Houston with a hundred dollar haircut and a beach house once featured in *Southern Living* called and wanted me to help investigate the complaints of so-called Gulf War veterans the media had named "Gulf War Syndrome." My Birmingham law firm had played a minor role in one of his mass tort cases.

The lawyer told me he'd interviewed two dozen Gulf War veterans, most of them women, and that he and some biologist had a theory that Gulf War syndrome was caused by a bacteriological agent invented in the United States and sold by this country to Iraq when it looked as though Iran was winning its war with Iraq. The bug was manufactured from part of the AIDS virus, he added.

I asked Mr. Haircut, Esquire, how many regular Marine officers he'd interviewed. He was silent for twenty seconds. Then he said, "Well just because these victims are female. . . ."

"How many female regular Army Rangers, officers or enlisted personnel, have you interviewed?" I said.

There was another long pause. "Well, most of these ladies are reservists or members of National Guard units," he said.

"Yeah, that's what I thought," I said. "I appreciate your calling, but I don't think I'm interested."

I wondered briefly whether in Michael Godchaux I had encountered another Mr. Haircut.

The damp Southeastern weather had deteriorated since my flight down to New Orleans. The ceiling was now one thousand overcast, and a light rain was falling on Lake Pontchartrain. No safe choice but to file IFR and climb above the liquid atmosphere. Fortunately, the cloud tops were only at nine thousand feet, about two minutes of climbing through the gunk in the Albatros if the Houston Air Route Traffic Control Center would allow me the uninterrupted climb.

The ARTCC controller nixed my proposed flight plan to go direct to flight level one eight zero and required me to hold at nine thousand feet. Turbulence would lurk at the horizontal condensation boundary.

I read back the amended clearance and taxied out to the hold-short line. I was number two for takeoff behind a Cessna Citation I that had seen better days.

One minute after takeoff and just after the tower handed me off to Center, the controller in Houston gave me approval to continue to eighteen thousand feet. I broke out into bright winter sunshine around nine thousand feet, rode a few bumps there and continued to the lowest of the flight levels.

A few minutes later, I was handed off to Atlanta, and by then it was time to start down. I was cleared to descend in a series of steps and a couple of turns until I came dripping down out of the low clouds on the ILS approach to runway two-four in Birmingham. I landed, and, since no aircraft were holding for takeoff, I used air braking to save the brakes, holding the nose wheel off the centerline down to fifty knots.

Back in the FBO, I texted Sally again. She was home on the Southside, and, having little else to accomplish on a Sunday afternoon, I stopped at the hotel, picked up my running shoes and gear, a change of clothes, and on impulse, red carnations at the gift shop, and drove to her place.

Warm and filled with midday light, Sally's condo felt like a haven from the cold, damp day.

"Hey," Sally said when she opened the door.

"Hey yourself." I handed her the carnations. "Here. For you."

"Thanks! Carnations. Love them. My father used to wear a white one in his lapel sometimes. Aren't you coming in?"

"I suppose I might," I said.

Sally filled a crystal vase with water for the carnations. "There. Not just for me," she said. "For us." Barefoot, she wore an Alabama Southern sweatsuit and, I soon discovered, nothing else. We spent the next two hours in her bedroom.

Afterwards, I made a late lunch for us, shrimp salad, goat cheese, and cranberry crackers Sally had bought at the Whole Foods store. We sat at her little bar to eat while I gave her a general outline of the Michael Godchaux meeting.

"I've been thinking while you've been jousting about the South," Sally said. "You know it's not as though I don't have a stake here. One of my girls is missing, another dead, and you know about my relationship with Don. You asked me why I said what I said in the dorm. 'We have to get them.' Remember?"

"Yes."

"I do want to participate. I know I'm just a soccer coach, so tell me if I'm intruding, but I do have some questions about all this."

I nodded. "Understandable."

"So, why did you go to New Orleans today?"

I explained the purpose of my visit to the Crescent City without naming Michael Godchaux.

Sally frowned. "So, how is this person related to Kris Kramer's disappearance, exactly?"

"I barely know whether it's related vaguely. Much less exactly. But I do know Don Kramer was working on a big case involving the oil business and politicians on the take. Maybe payoffs from the New Orleans Mob. And I know somebody sent muscle to try to scare me off. That's the style of that sort of crowd. I'm just pulling on strings. Somewhere there's a string connected to Kris Kramer."

"And someone killed Akilah."

"Yes."

"Same someone?"

"I'm sure that question has occurred to the police. I'm just trying to concentrate on finding Kris."

"I appreciate that. It's just. . . ."

"What?"

Sally hugged herself and shook her head slowly from side to side. "Don led a . . . a complicated life. He worked on more than one legal matter. When I was with him, he'd take calls from people. Not just related to his law practice. Politicians. College friends. Lawyers he'd met traveling for cases. People he'd met in bars. All sorts."

"I think I understand. I should not approach this with tunnel vision. Could be related to some other case."

Sally shrugged. "Just keep pulling on those threads."

We finished eating, mostly in silence. As the dark afternoon grew darker, the rain began again, a steady downpour that didn't look as though it might abate for hours.

Sally collected the plates and rinsed them and placed them in her dishwasher. She came around behind me, leaned her head on my back, and spoke softly into my neck. "You don't really want to go back to that convention hotel tonight, do you? After all, if you're concerned about my safety, what better protection could I have than your presence?" she said.

I didn't want to spend another night in a convention hotel, not this night, not any night. "Actually, I see no reason to go back there at all except to pack my bags and check out."

"And stay here for . . . for the duration?"

"What saves a man is to take a step," I said. "Saint-Exupery."

"It seems like the right step to me if it does to you," Sally said. "Sally Kronenberg."

I couldn't argue with Saint-Exupery and Kronenberg. I called the hotel and told them I would be checking out this afternoon, then drove to the hotel, collected my things, checked out, and moved in with Sally.

CHAPTER TWENTY-FOUR

Monday January 30

Last night's rain had stopped after midnight. Dawn arrived gradually over Red Mountain, a smooth gray dome covering the Birmingham sky. Before Sally awoke, I sat on the cushion for fifteen minutes, then showered and made a breakfast of eggs, whole wheat toast, and coffee.

As I finished cooking, Sally walked out of the bedroom in a white satin robe. "I woke up and smelled coffee," she said. "I'm hungry. Did you make enough for both of us?"

"Two of us here, aren't there?" I set out plates and napkins and served the food while Sally poured coffee, and we ate together in silence like an old married couple.

Chewing her last bite of toast, Sally gestured toward my zabuton and bolster, which I had stowed in a corner beside the windows with the view of the mountain. "Were you doing yoga?" she asked.

"Not exactly." I explained that I tried to meditate a few minutes every day.

"So, are you a Buddhist?" she asked.

Tempted as I was to say "Not exactly" again, I had come to recognize such an answer for the dodge it is, particularly in the deep South, where it seems at least at first glance that the only categories of religious views recognized by most are Baptist, Episcopalian, Holy Roller and atheist. Only the broad-minded recognized Catholics and Jews. That's a vast oversimplification of a North American region where religious practices – did I mention snake handlers? – are as varied and complicated as they are anywhere but India.

Nevertheless, I sometimes dodged the question, but this did not need to be one of those times. "Yes," I answered. "I suppose I am."

"You're an interesting man, Slate."

"I don't know about that." I forked up my last bite of egg, picked up the plates and turned to the sink, my back to Sally. "I sort of walked through the back gate of meditation and discovered, inside, the garden of Buddhism.

"I didn't grow up going to church every Sunday like so many Southerners. My parents weren't atheists, and I'm not sure they'd ever met a Buddhist, but my grandparents forced them to spend so much time in redneck churches that they had a bellyful of Southern-fried religion by the time they were grown. So they didn't take me to church much.

"After my wife and son died, I started seeing a psychiatrist here in Birmingham, at UAB. Dr. Beverly Adams. I don't have many family members and few close friends, and I needed to talk to someone.

"Anyway. Of course Dr. Adams is also a medical doctor, and she would always take my blood pressure before we started to talk. After a couple of sessions, she suggested I try meditation because my pressure was above normal. I read a couple of books and started on my own, just sitting in the floor in the morning for a few minutes. More reading led me to a few books about Buddhism. The title of the first one might describe me: *The Accidental Buddhist*. Then I discovered that right here in Birmingham a real Tibetan monk trained by the Dalai Lama himself had started a Tibetan Buddhist center. I visited a few times, bought those cushions, and started mediating thirty minutes morning and evening."

"So, did your blood pressure come down?"

"About twenty points. I started working out more too, but I think the pressure drop was mostly attributable to meditation.

"So that's pretty much the whole story. I'm still not sure Buddhism is exactly a religion. No creator deity. The Dalai Lama himself admits that Buddhism may be more properly characterized as a philosophy."

I placed the last of the dishes in the dishwasher. "Anyway, it works for me so far."

"That's pretty cool," Sally said. "And now I want to amend interesting to fascinating." She stood. "We'll talk more later. But now I have to get ready for work."

Sally gave me her spare key, and I gave her a lingering kiss goodbye. She finally pushed me away and scooted for the shower. I left the apartment, locked the door with my new key, and headed downtown for my conference with Bill Woolf.

Since the interview with Godchaux, I knew that, no matter how or why the memory stick had come into the possession of the starting goalkeeper on the Alabama Southern women's soccer team, the electronic files arguably constituted the work product of Kramer and of his law firm. Even though I wanted to trade the information in those files for the use of the FBI's computer experts and their work product and for whatever the FBI might know about Mr. Godchaux of New Orleans, no way would I share information that might waive the work product privilege in a lawsuit. The work product privilege shielded information from discovery when that information derived from or tended to reveal the thoughts and mental impressions of counsel. A court would order such information revealed only when the party seeking it could show that no other means of obtaining the information existed.

I arrived at Woolf White at seven-thirty on the dot. A deposition was already underway in the large conference room off the lobby, and the lobby receptionist/legal assistant/switchboard operator, busy as an air traffic controller, chattered into her headset. Bill Woolf walked out of the deposition, legal pad in hand. "What can I do for you, Slate?"

I asked him if we could step into his office. "Back here," he said, indicating the law library occupying the space adjacent to the foyer. The law library, like those of most large firms, served these days as a place for lawyers to concentrate, or, in truth, as a visual reminder for clients of all the impressive knowledge their fees bought. The books themselves were as anachronistic as illuminated manuscripts.

We stood among the volumes while I explained the issue. "Got it," Woolf said. "Find out if we have a joint prosecution agreement with the government in the *qui tam* case. If not, have the U.S. attorney send over the government's standard agreement. We could assert the joint prosecution privilege without it, but let's have it in hand. That's all I need. Then give them the disk, or thumb drive, or whatever it is."

"Will do," I said.

"Thanks, Slate. If you need anything else, let me know. I have to get back to this deposition. Billable hours are calling me."

The day was still too fresh to expect to find an assistant U.S. attorney or an FBI agent at his or her desk, but I had another visit to make this morning.

The Birmingham city jail on Sixth Avenue South, a dozen blocks from Elmwood Cemetery, kept early hours for visitors. The jail personnel did not make appointments, and I had not been invited. Maybe Chief Grubbs' office would have called down to the jail if I had asked, so the guards would have Royal ready for my visit. And maybe not. I liked it better this way. The chances that Royal would agree to see me were pretty good, I thought. I also thought it might be a good idea for a guard to remain in the vicinity. Royal might want a little revenge.

The front door of the jail opened to a large, bleak waiting area: chipped, dirty beige paint, cheap plastic chairs along the walls, drink and snack machines in one corner. Families and friends were camped out waiting on other relatives, hoping for a five-minute visit with a prisoner: wives and girlfriends and children; grandmothers and grandkids; uncles, aunts, cousins; homies, brothers, sisters; two-year-olds playing in a corner with blocks; babies on laps.

Behind a window of thick glass set into a metal wall in one corner, a uniformed guard, a woman, African-American, heavy-set and unsmiling, sat at the sign-in desk for visitors. After I ran the gauntlet in the waiting room, she handed me a clipboard with a ratty photocopied sign-in sheet attached. I filled in Royal's name and the time of my visit. For the purpose of my visit and relationship to the inmate, I wrote the single word: "lawyer." Not exactly right. Not exactly wrong. A lawyer's response.

"Since you're a lawyer, Mr. Slate, we'll bring him up to the library," the guard said. "And you can come on back."

The metal door at the end of the corridor created by the cage for the sign-in guard made a metallic click as I neared it, and a buzzer sounded. I pulled open the door and stepped into another corridor about fifteen feet long and four feet wide, sheathed in metal walls, with a heavy metal door at each end, the first of which I had just been buzzed through.

"Walk on," a voice instructed me.

As I approached the second door, the same buzzer sounded, the door clicked, and I walked out into a short concrete block hallway painted a lighter shade of beige. Running perpendicular to this hallway was an immense hall of concrete block and linoleum tile, with harsh fluorescent lighting and no windows.

A door twenty feet away opened and another uniformed guard, who looked big and strong enough to play offensive guard for the Saints, strode toward me, his rubber-soled shoes squeaking on the tile floor. "Mr. Slate?" he said. "You here to see prisoner Royal?"

I nodded.

"Follow me," he said.

I turned to my left and followed the guard down the hall about fifty feet to a door bearing a black and white "Library" sign. "Right in here," the guard said. "Prisoner Royal is being escorted down. Should be just a few minutes."

The jail's "library" consisted of a couple of flimsy folding tables, half a dozen cheap plastic chairs like the ones in the lobby, and maybe a hundred books on one shelving unit. Most of the books were out-of-date law books that appeared to have been donated by law firms: a partial set of the Alabama Code, a few volumes of the Alabama Digest, random volumes of the United States Code; three or four Bibles of the sort found in cheap hotel rooms.; a battered Merriam-Webster dictionary.

I sat at one of the tables to wait.

A few minutes turned out to be fifteen. I could not get a data or phone signal – too much metal and concrete in the building, and maybe too many antennas on the roof.

Finally, the door opened and I stood while the guard led in Royal, shackled at the wrists and ankles. The chains made a not-so-unpleasant rattle.

"I'll be right outside," the guard said. He went out and closed the door.

Royal looked at me from under his unibrow and gestured a little with his shackled hands. "So?" he said. "You wanted to see me. Want to hit me some more? Or you got somethin' to say?"

"Thanks for agreeing to see me," I said. "I wasn't sure you would."

"Hey. Anything to get away from the bloods a few minutes."

"Whatever. Look, I just wanted to ask you a few questions. Let's sit down for a minute. Okay?"

He shrugged. "Sure."

We sat across from each other at the table. I noticed a two-inch-square white bandage on the back of his right hand. "How's the hand?" I said.

"Not too bad. Still a little sore."

"Look, Billy," I said. "I don't know you. Didn't know you before you showed up at my hotel room door. 'Room Service,' right?"

Royal shrugged again. "It's worked before."

"I'm sure it has. And, just so I know, you never heard of me before, either. Right?"

"Nope."

"So, how'd you get the job?"

"Guy I know, called me, said to show up at the hotel and meet a guy."

"Who called you?"

"Like I said, a guy."

"A guy sometimes calls you for this kind of work?"

"You got it."

"Name?"

Royal shook his head. "I'll be out of this place in a couple days, soon as my bail hearing, which I hear is tomorrow. But if I told you a name, I might not ever leave."

172

"So, this guy told you to meet a guy at the hotel."

"You've been listenin'."

"I do that. Where in the hotel?"

"Bar." Royal shook his head. "Nobody in there but the one guy."

"How were you supposed to get paid?"

"Cash. Half then, half when I was done."

"Done with what?"

"Breakin' ribs, bustin' a head. Tellin' you to get out of the 'ham."

"Anything else you were supposed to tell me?"

"I was supposed to say, 'the oil business is none of your business.'"

"That's all? Just, 'the oil business is none of your business'?"

Royal nodded. "That was it."

"Nothing about a girl? Missing girl?"

"What?"

"You weren't supposed to tell me to lay off trying to find a young woman who's missing?"

Royal shook his head slowly. "I swear to you I don't know a damn thing about no missing girl."

It was my turn to shake my head. "Okay. What did this guy look like?"

"I don't know. Just a guy."

"Big guy?"

"Not as tall as me. Kinda thick though."

"Hair?"

"Yeah, he had hair."

"Come on. Dark hair, white guy, black guy, what?"

Royal sighed. "I don't know this guy, see. And I don't think he knows me. So I don't really care. He's a white guy, kinda thick like I said, dark hair, dark complexion. Brown eyes. Say," he said.

"Yeah?"

"You know that TV show they used to have on HBO? What was it? That Mafia show?"

"*The Sopranos?*"

"Yeah. *The Sopranos.* Used to watch that show all the time. This guy looked just like that guy on the Sopranos, what was his name? Tony Sopranos. Yeah. That's it. That's kinda how he looked. Italian, you know."

"Okay Billy. I appreciate your speaking with me."

"I wish you'd tell the judge. Go easy on me, you know? I got an ex-wife and a couple kids in Walker County, you know?"

I nodded. "Yeah, I know, Billy." I held out my hand, and he reached up to shake, wincing a little, the chain between his wrists dragging across the table.

I stood and opened the door, then closed it and turned back. "I don't suppose you were the guy sent to trash my boat, were you?" I asked Royal.

"You got a boat?" he said. "Bass boat? Pontoon?"

"For what it's worth, it's a sailboat," I said.

Royal shook his head. "I don't know nothin' about your boat."

"Okay, Billy," I said. "I guess that's all."

I opened the door. The guard was leaning against the wall to the left. "All done?" he said.

"For now," I said.

"Okay," he said. Just walk back up the corridor and stand at the door where you came through. The officers in reception will see you and let you out."

Unless Billy Royal was lying – and he wasn't smart enough for that – he'd never give me the connection between the oil and gas case and Kris Kramer. Maybe there was no connection. Maybe there was no connection between Kramer's death and the oil and gas case, no connection between Don Kramer's murder and Kris Kramer's kidnapping. Maybe there were two, or even three, separate cases.

And maybe tomorrow the skies would be sunny and the temperature seventy-five. But that was not the way to bet.

In the waiting room, the families didn't seem to have moved. The grannies and mamas and kids seemed so dispirited, so enervated, that no one had the energy to glare at me for getting in and out before they could see their husbands or boyfriends or sons. Nor did any of them seem ready to volunteer the answers I needed.

Outside, the same gray helmet sat tight over the Birmingham sky, with damp cold air but no rain.

CHAPTER TWENTY-FIVE

Sitting in the car in the parking lot at the jail, I called Bill Alston. His voice mail suggested that I leave a message at the beep, so I told him that I had an object in which he had expressed some interest and wondered whether he would be up for an exchange.

Alston called me back before I got to Twentieth Street. "Hey sport," he said. "Where have you been keeping yourself? Thought I'd hear from you after the big meet with the lawyers."

"I had a few other things to do," I said.

"Travel is broadening, they say."

"They do say that. But why do you think I've been traveling?"

You forgot I'm from the government, and I'm here to watch, I mean to help, you," Alston said.

So much for flying under the radar. I might as well have sent FBI director Bob Mueller an email with my itinerary for the year. "Right. So.

Maybe we can help each other. I have something you'd like to see. Why don't we meet for coffee somewhere?"

"Just say when and where, sport. We live to serve."

"How about Safari Cup on Third Avenue North in ten minutes?"

"Make it fifteen. Okay if Agent Sanders joins us?"

"Not a problem. I forgot fibbies always travel in pairs. See you there."

I parked in the deck next to the City Federal Building and walked through a muddy alley, dodging puddles lingering from last night's rain, and around the corner and across the street to the coffee shop. The two special agents were drinking coffee and eating pastries at a wrought-iron table for four with a marble top near the big floor-to-ceiling windows overlooking Twenty-First Street.

Alston saw me and waved as I entered the shop. I nodded and got into the line for coffee. When it was my turn, I ordered a medium Kenya dark roast. The server, a slim man in his late twenties with a blond soul patch and two gold loops in his left ear, asked if I wanted space for milk. I told him I did. When the coffee came, I had him add a half-inch of hot skim milk and then slid down the bar to the station where they kept sweeteners. I grabbed two packets of Equal and a wooden stirring stick and walked slowly over to the FBI agents' table, careful not to spill the hot coffee.

"Solved any crimes today, Slate?" Alston asked before I sat down.

"No, but it's early," I said. Taking off my rain parka and draping it over a chair, I sat next to Sanders and across from Alston. I took a long slow sip of coffee. "Coffee's great here," I said.

"Doughnuts aren't bad either," Alston allowed.

"You're all cop," I said.

"I like to think so," he said.

Sanders rolled her eyes. "If you guys are finished with the male bonding good-old-boy routine, can we transact some of the people's business here?" she said.

Alston shrugged. "If we must. Slate, we hear you may have made a decision about the thumb drive."

I took another sip of coffee. "That depends," I said.

Sanders looked sideways at me. "You are hardly in a position to bargain with us, are you?" she said.

"Let's just listen to what Slate has to say, Agent Sanders," Alston said. "What is it you want from us, Slate?"

"Three things. First, access to all the information your lab guys pull off the drive. Second, I want the device back undamaged and unchanged."

"Well, as I understand it, the device belongs to the Woolf White firm. I assume you speak for them?" Alston said.

"On this matter, I do."

"We'll have someone call Bill Woolf to confirm that. But, assuming that's true, then I see no problem with those conditions."

Alston picked up the last crumb of his doughnut with an index finger, put it to his mouth, and took a sip of coffee. "So, now, on to door number three. What else do you need from us, Slate?"

"Information. Have you heard of a man named Michael Godchaux?"

The two agents looked at each other for the first time since I had sat down.

"Godchaux is a fairly common name in Louisiana, isn't it?" Sanders asked.

"Used to be a big sugar mill, sold retail sugar as Godchaux Sugar, I think." Alston said.

"Closed down in nineteen eighty-five," Sanders said.

The agents glanced at each other again. Alston nodded slightly. "We know Michael Godchaux," Sanders said.

"And he has nothing to do with the defunct Godchaux Sugar," I said.

"Nope," Sanders said.

"Well," I said. "That's a start. What else do you know?"

"You visited our Mr. Godchaux." It was Alston.

I breathed in and out. A swinging gate. "I guessed that you knew that when we spoke on the phone a few minutes ago. Maybe we can do it this way. How long have you known Godchaux?"

Agent Sanders stood and said, "I'm getting a refill. Need anything?" She looked at Alston but, pointedly I thought, not at me.

Alston watched her walk away and then leaned toward me, elbows on the marble table, coffee cup circled in his big hands. "Michael Godchaux, as I think you know, is the relator in the *qui tam* case Don Kramer was working on."

He took a sip of coffee. "Look, this is all confidential. I know you understand that, Slate, but you must tell me you will not reveal the information I am going to give to you. I'm a lawyer too, you know, even if I am just a lowly FBI agent. Lawyer to lawyer. Okay?"

I told him I agreed.

"Good." He leaned forward a little more. "In addition to being a relator, Godchaux is a confidential informant. He walked into the offices of the United States attorney in New Orleans, four years ago next month. He demanded that he would speak only with the United States attorney for the Eastern District of Louisiana. It so happened that the U.S. attorney was in his office. Once the interview began, Godchaux agreed that a couple of FBI agents could sit in. The U.S. attorney rearranged his schedule, brought in sandwiches for lunch. My boss at that time, the head of the New Orleans FBI office, and I were the two agents."

"So your last post was New Orleans?"

"That's right," Alston said as Sanders sat back down. He nodded at her. "Since then, Godchaux has been one of my responsibilities. Even after I transferred here to Birmingham, I kept that task because Godchaux trusted me and because he had begun to give us information relevant to the Alabama oil leases that you already know about."

"So why did you need me and this thumb drive?"

"Huh. You met Godchaux. He's my informant, but he's a squirrely dude. He realized pretty soon after he began to give us information that he could also be a relator in a civil *qui tam* case. That's when he contacted Don Kramer."

"Godchaux doesn't tell Bill everything," Sanders said.

"Not by a long shot he doesn't." Alston nodded.

"So Godchaux found Kramer, not the other way around," I said.

"Not the usual way with plaintiffs' lawyers, but I believe that is what happened here," Alston said.

"And he played you both?" I asked.

Sanders sighed. "I don't mean to be critical of our man. Michael Godchaux is very bright, very capable. He has provided us with a mother lode of good, accurate information. The Alabama case is important, but it is not the major part of the government's investigation into the involvement of organized crime in small oil and gas businesses in the South. We're close to indictments here and in Louisiana."

"That could explain a CI's being a little squirrely, or, charitably, a little nervous," I said.

"It could," Sanders said. "I would be."

"Anyway," said Alston. "I don't know what information is on that thumb drive. It could be data we already have. It could be something entirely new. It could be something Godchaux wanted to share only with Kramer. I mean, you know, before."

"Before the kidnapping, before Kramer's death."

"One or both."

"Speaking of which, let me ask both of you your opinion about something else," I said.

"Opinions I share freely, sport. Facts are another matter."

"Yeah. Well. Here it is. Do you think Kris Kramer's kidnapping is related to her father's work?"

"What else?" Sanders asked.

"That's been our assumption," Alston said. "If you have some other angle or thought or information, we'd like to hear it."

I shook my head. "No. No facts. No theories. I just want to make sure I'm keeping an open mind."

Sanders spoke. "I think we have all finished our coffee now." She looked at me. "Where is the memory stick, Slate?"

"Before we get to that, I do have one other question."

When neither agent responded, I asked, "Has Godchaux been compromised?"

Alston shook his head slowly. "You mean, do his former employers know about his discussions with us?"

I nodded yes.

"We have no reason to think so. After all, he's still healthy. There's been no contact with the former employer that we know about. And besides. . . ."

"Besides?"

"I mentioned Godchaux is a little squirrely. Uses disguises. Very savvy about technology. Even we have difficulty listening in on that guy. When he walked into the U.S. attorney's office? Security video shows a blonde woman entering the building about five minutes before Godchaux was buzzed in to the outer office. The woman goes into a public restroom on the first floor. Michael Godchaux walks out of the restroom a few minutes later. No," he said, shaking his head emphatically. "They don't know."

I stood, put on my rain parka, unzipped the inside pocket, pulled out the memory stick, and proffered the device to Sanders. "Here you go," I said.

Sanders stared up at me. "You're a cool dude, aren't you?"

"I try," I said.

Alston's shoulders were shaking, but he managed not to laugh out loud.

"And you will need something else," I said. "May I borrow a pen?"

Alston pulled a ballpoint out of a shirt pocket. "Here you go, sport," he said.

I unfolded the cocktail napkin under Sanders' coffee mug and wrote the password on the reverse side. "Remember our deal," I said.

"You'll be first with the information outside the government," Alston promised.

I shot him with a forefinger. "You're the man," I said. I made my way to the rear exit, into the main lobby of the Title Building, and through its revolving door and out into the cold damp air.

CHAPTER TWENTY-SIX

"**R**emember I told you the autopsy and other forensic evidence indicated Kramer was not killed where the body was found?" Grubbs asked.

"I remember," I said.

"Now we know where." Grubbs passed me an eleven-by-fourteen color print of a concrete stairwell painted white, the white dribbled with dark red. I'd taken a chance Grubbs would be in his office when I finished with Tweedledum and Tweedledee, and I'd walked the five blocks to Grubbs' office.

Grubbs continued while I looked at the photograph. "Maintenance employees at the Park Plaza noticed something looked different in one of the parking deck stairwells before they started some scheduled power washing this weekend. The discoloring on the wall is a bloodstain. The type matches Kramer's. We're waiting for DNA confirmation, but I'm willing to take the bet that this is the site of the murder."

"Anything else?"

"No casings or fragments in the walls. That would be consistent with the autopsy, which found that Kramer was killed by one bullet which entered approximately one centimeter to the midline of the posterior skull and did not exit."

"Is that part of the deck covered by a security camera?"

"No. That stairwell is just outside the line of sight of the nearest one, which covers the east side of the third floor of the deck."

I tossed the print back across the desk. "So. Anything else?"

"There is some video from inside the building. A white man wearing a dark suit and a dark raincoat, with a fedora pulled down over his eyes, rode the elevator to Woolf White's floor around five-thirty that afternoon. He got off the elevator and apparently walked down the corridor to the men's room. You probably know that building is configured so that all offices on each floor share men's and women's restrooms on central halls coming in each direction off the elevator lobby. Even on floors where one business rents the entire floor, the configuration is the same."

"Guy was wearing a hat? Changes the look."

"Yep. You show a witness photos of a guy without a hat, if they saw him wearing a hat, they'll swear it's different guys. Of course, it was raining that day. Maybe explains the hat.

"We had prints made of the best still capture of the man's face from the video. Showed them around in the building. No one recognizes this guy.

"Kramer walks out to the elevators at five fifty-two. Our man appears in the elevator lobby just as the car arrives, and he gets on the elevator with Kramer. They ride down to the third floor. As the elevator opens, you can see them talking. Kramer looks animated, waves his arms a bit; the unidentified guy looks calm. They both get off the elevator and head for the parking garage door.

"And that's all we've got. No one saw this guy follow Kramer out of the building. Apparently, there is a camera in the area where the parking deck door is located, sort of around behind the elevator lobby, but it wasn't working that day."

"No video in the elevator?"

"That wasn't working either."

"Without an identification, this doesn't help much," I said.

"No, it does not. FBI is running the stills through their new facial recognition software. Birmingham is not part of the trial they're running on this system, but this case rated high priority because of the unusual circumstance of a kidnapping and murder in the same family just days apart."

"With any luck, maybe they'll get a hit."

"Have you been lucky lately? I personally have not. They tell me this technology is in its early stages, and it's useless if a face or some other biometric identifier, like a fingerprint, is not in the database. But at least, I'm told, this software is not fooled by somebody wearing a hat."

"Okay. Waiting for the FBI is what I do, lately. But also, how did the body get moved? Assuming this is the killer, assuming Kramer was killed in the stairwell outside the parking deck, how did the killer get the body down to the rail yards without being seen? Teleportation?"

"If the bad guys have that, I'm taking early retirement," Grubbs said.

"There had to be a car," I said.

"I believe so," Grubbs nodded.

"But how did the killer get the body in a car trunk or a back seat without getting caught on video?"

"That is a question I've been rolling around in my head." He shrugged. "Some of the cameras were not working."

"So, nothing else so far?"

"Nope. That's why I decided to tell you. Thought you might meditate about it and come up with something."

I smiled. "You should try it, dude. Works wonders on the blood pressure."

"So I hear. Maybe I will."

I stood, turned, opened the office door, and turned back toward Grubbs. "I appreciate the info," I said. "See you around."

"Slate," Grubbs said. I turned back. "Find the girl," he said. "I'm getting tired of the press conferences."

I nodded and left without another word.

Find the girl. Find the girl. Find the girl. The phrase pulsed through my head like a mantra as I walked back to the City Federal parking garage in the weak midday light. I had thought this case would begin and end in January. Now, nearing a new month, I didn't feel much closer to the end than to the beginning.

As to finding Kris Kramer, I had done, or actually failed to do, something which, if acted on by my enemies – I had a few – could result in my indictment for obstruction of justice. I had not, not yet anyway, told either the Birmingham Police Department or the FBI about the note on the old computer on my boat. The FBI knew my boat had been searched, thanks to Agent Sanders' flirtation with Moeller, but I hadn't even told Moeller about the note.

In my defense, I had a defense. I'm a lawyer, Kramer was my client, and the information related to the matter for which Kramer hired me. The privilege survives the client's death, but the information I had failed to disclose was not obtained through a communication with the client. I hadn't told anyone at all about the note, not even Susan Kramer, who was arguably also my client, especially after the meeting in Woolf White's offices. Not telling her might be tantamount to something akin to failure to communicate a settlement offer to a client, and thus run afoul of the Alabama Rules of Professional Conduct. That is, if a putative communication purporting to be from a kidnapper amounted to a settlement offer. I had not been certain at the time of the communication that Susan Kramer was my client, but something else, something besides my normal reserve, must have prevented me from telling her about the digital note.

At least I had not assisted anyone with committing a crime. To my knowledge.

On the other hand, whoever had written the note had not gotten back in touch, except through his emissary, Billy Royal.

I should have confided in Moeller. He would have generated ideas. Maybe his ideas would have been better than his efforts to find the password for the thumb drive.

But it wasn't too late, at least not to speak with Moeller. Before I started the car, I called Moeller and asked if I could once again rent his mind for a couple of hours for the price of a dinner at Hemingway's. If it was about the memory stick, he said, he would pass. I told him how I'd obtained the password and how the FBI code breakers were at work on the contents of the files. I told him I just wanted to lay out the facts for him and to have him think through them to see where they should lead as a matter of logic.

"It's always easiest, Slate, to just ask someone for the password, isn't it?" Moeller said.

I admitted that had turned out to be true. I told him I'd be at the restaurant by six-thirty, and he told me I was his for the evening.

I texted Sally, "Seafood dinner tonight?" and she texted back "Yes!!!" I told her we needed to leave the condo by five. I didn't tell her we'd be traveling by high-performance jet. She deserved a surprise or two.

At Sally's place, I changed into running clothes and went for a forty-minute run along Clairmont Avenue. Back at the condo, I showered, ate two bagels with smoked salmon, and drank a cup of peppermint tea. I sat on my cushion for thirty minutes, then checked the aviation weather and called the FBO and asked them to tow the Albatros out of the hangar and make sure it was fueled and ready to fly. Hemingway's was happy to make a reservation for three on a Monday night in late January for any time we wanted to arrive.

I spent the remainder of the afternoon creating a timeline, a document I should have kept on a day-to-day basis after Kramer had visited me in Gulf Shores, to review with Moeller and Sally after dinner. When I practiced law, I had followed the advice of my senior litigation partner and created a timeline for every lawsuit, a document that expanded in both temporal directions as discovery proceeded in the case. Forcing myself to adopt this discipline meant I usually had better recall of the facts than my opponent, a priceless advantage in depositions, and in court.

Sally returned to the condo a little after four. I suggested that appropriate attire for the evening could be jeans, boots, a sweater, and a warm jacket, and that she might need to pack a small overnight bag in case the weather deteriorated. She gave me a curious smile, showered, and changed into black jeans, a black turtleneck sweater, motorcycle boots, and a black leather jacket. Throwing a change of clothes and a few essentials into a bag took five minutes. My kind of girl.

Driving to the airport, we stayed on surface roads, but the drive took fifteen minutes longer than usual in the afternoon traffic.

The Birmingham airport is not located in one of the better neighborhoods in town. As we cruised through the Lakeview district, Sally said, "So has Frank Stitt opened a new place in Avondale?"

I smirked. "Not that I've heard of."

Closer to the airport, Sally asked, "So you're taking me to a restaurant in Concourse C?"

Gourmet food at the Birmingham airport is putting hot mustard on your pre-made turkey sandwich. "Not exactly," I said.

I parked outside the FBO, pulled my flight gear out of the trunk, and said, "Follow me, babe." We walked through the FBO and out onto the ramp. The Albatros, gleaming under the bright ramp lights, sat no more than fifty feet from the FBO's doors.

"This is yours?" Sally said.

"Yep," I answered. "We're flying to the coast for fresh seafood. In an hour we'll be eating gumbo with hot sauce and crackers."

"I'm ready!" she said.

I handed Sally my extra David Clark headset, climbed up to the rear cockpit, opened the hatch, then jumped down and showed Sally how to use the two steps up. She stood on the seat, and I climbed up and helped her sit down, strap in, and plug in her headset. I climbed back down and did a preflight walk-around. Sally gave a me a thumbs-up sign as I checked the right-side fuel cap.

Finished with the pre-flight, I climbed up to the front cockpit, strapped in, turned on the master and avionics switches, and spoke to Sally on the intercom. "Are you still up for this? I sort of threw you into the rear seat of a high-performance jet without much explanation. If you like flying, you'll love it. If not, we can always get a turkey sandwich over in Concourse C."

"No sir, Mr. Slate," she said. "I'm looking forward to fresh blackened redfish tonight."

"Okay, then. Here we go." I showed Sally how to close and lock her canopy and called clearance delivery for an IFR clearance and transponder code. I went through the engine start sequence, and in less than a minute, the little jet was whistling and almost ready to fly. We taxied out and waited for takeoff sequencing behind a Delta MD-88 and a Falcon 50.

As the Falcon taxied into position for takeoff and we took our place at the hold-short line, I reached down and turned the volume on the intercom all the way down. I've done that every time I've given someone his or her first ride in the Albatros. Inevitably, either at the beginning of the takeoff roll when the little jet gathers itself and begins its rush down the runway like a runaway G-sled, or just after wheels-up and best climb speed is reached and I point the nose at the sky, the new rider finds it impossible to maintain the sterile cockpit rule I've tried to impose and simply has to scream in delight or terror or both.

The tower had traffic moving, with late afternoon flights stacked deep, as they were at even moderately busy airports like Birmingham. By the time the Falcon lifted its nosewheel, the controller gave us a position and hold clearance, and when the Falcon pilot raised the landing gear a moment after takeoff, she gave us our takeoff clearance.

Climbing through three thousand feet, I turned the intercom back on. "Still along for the ride back there?" I said.

"Did you hear me scream?" I could hear the broad smile if I couldn't see it. "I couldn't stop myself."

The clouds had lifted and parted just enough to create a fish-scale sunset, pinks and oranges filling the sky to our right as we flew almost due south at ten thousand feet.

The sunset faded and darkness fell as we approached Mobile Bay and the Alabama Gulf coast. The lights of Mobile and the eastern shore guided us down the mouth of the bay and inland for a visual approach to runway nine at Jack Edwards airport. The tires chirped on the asphalt, and soon we were loaded into the airport courtesy car for the fifteen-minute drive down Highway 59 South, then east on Route 98 to Orange Beach and the marina.

We would not have needed a reservation at Hemingway's on this Monday at the end of January. No bleaker month shared the calendar in Alabama.

At the bar sat Hans Moeller, nursing a Scotch with two ice cubes and chatting up the bartender, a woman in her mid-twenties with thick waist-length brown hair. She wore a low-cut plaid jumper with a band of creamy lace at the collar, if a band dipping between her breasts could be considered a collar.

Moeller saw me in the mirror behind the bar – not all of his attention was on the bartender – and swiveled to greet me. "Slate!" he said. "Just in time. I'm afraid I have been overselling the merits of a Caribbean cruise on a small motorsailer named for a Swiss hero."

The bartender smiled. "Overselling the merits of spending a month on a boat with Hans Moeller, more like."

Moeller shrugged. "At least she remembers my name. Think about it, my dear," he said.

"But, Slate, you – you're not alone. Well." He looked Sally up and down, then smiled brightly at me. "It's a long road that knows no turning."

I gestured toward Sally. "Sally Kronenberg, meet my friend Hans Moeller. Hans, Sally Kronenberg."

Sally reached out to shake Moeller's hand, but he took her hand in his and brought it to his lips. *"Guten Abend, Fraulein.* Surely a woman named Kronenberg speaks German, *nein?"*

"Eine kleine," Sally said. "My grandparents immigrated from Heidelberg, but no one in the family thought to speak German to me when I was young."

"Hah. You are still young, *mein liebe,* believe me." He turned to me. "Holding out on me, Slate?"

"Just busy. Let's get a table. Anyone hungry?"

Sally said, "I'm starving. I think flying fighter planes does that to me."

On the dock side of the restaurant, behind the bar, the dining room, captain's chairs and bare wood tables in dark oak, overlooked the harbor. Over each table hung a light in the shape of a ship's wheel. A lobster tank sat bubbling in one corner.

There were only three couples in the dining room. We chose a window table away from the others. Sally and I dropped our bags near our table along the wall under the window.

Seated, Moeller appraised Sally and me, a small smile playing at the corners of his mouth. "If this were a better establishment, I'd order a round of Kronenbourg 1664, but I'm afraid the only European beer on tap is Irish, not German."

"Most popular lager in France," Sally said. "Founded in Strasbourg."

"Should be a German city, but the Frogs claim it now," Moeller said.

The waitress interrupted them to take drink orders. Moeller ordered another Scotch, Sally a Grey Goose martini.

I had thought we might return to Birmingham after dinner, but Sally and Moeller had forced me into defensive drinking. I would never fly after drinking, and the FAA rule is eight hours between your last drink and piloting an aircraft. Eight hours bottle to throttle. Not long enough in my judgment, but nobody asked me.

"Manhattan on the rocks, Evan Williams Black." I touched Sally's hand. "Glad we made contingent overnight plans."

"Me too," she said.

"Slate's boat is not exactly the Ritz," Moeller offered, eyebrows raised a judicious millimeter. I could see where things were going with Moeller and realized that if I didn't slam on the brakes, he'd be at me with innuendo all evening. Besides, I needed his forebrain engaged, not the limbic system.

"You didn't tell me you lived on a boat," Sally said.

"I would've gotten around to it," I told her.

To Moeller I said, "Sally is a soccer coach. Kris Kramer's soccer coach. We met a few days ago. I asked her to dinner."

"And the rest, as they say. . . ."

"Is none of your business," I said.

"Sounds serious," Moeller said.

"'And the rest' is that Slate is now officially my sweet patootie," Sally said.

Our waitress brought our drinks; the conversation paused as we took in the calm dark water of the harbor.

When she had finished, Moeller said, "Oh. Now that explains everything. Why didn't you just say so, Slate?" He raised his glass. "To new love," he said.

"I'll drink to that," I said.

Sally touched our glasses. "*Prost!*" she said.

We started with cups of seafood gumbo, chunks of crab, whole shrimp and sausage in a thick brown broth, served in plain white ceramic bowls over rice. I ordered a Guinness; Moeller and Sally stayed with their first choices.

Gumbo is properly eaten with a brisk splash of Tabasco, with spoon in one hand and a saltine cracker, the square ones that come in cellophane two to a package, in the other.

After the gumbo, I ordered each of us a small West Indies salad, simple as diced onion and chunks of crabmeat marinated overnight in oil, vinegar, and ice water. A restaurant owner in Mobile named Bill Bayley invented the West Indies salad in 1947. Bayley and his restaurant are long gone, but the man should get more credit for the plain but elegant seafood that he served up at Bayley's Restaurant on Dauphin Island Parkway.

Offshore fishing in Alabama waters remains quite good through the winter. The fresh entrees were redfish, vermillion snapper and grouper. I ordered grouper Oscar, Sally, as promised, the blackened redfish. Moeller wanted grilled snapper. Shared bowls of steamed broccoli and asparagus served accompanied by tiny carafes of clarified butter and a loaf of French bread came to the table with the entrees.

After the gumbo and the salad – especially after the gumbo – I needed another Guinness. Moeller seemed to have some arrangement with management under which tumblers of Scotch with two ice cubes appeared as if on an assembly line. Sally drank Chardonnay with her redfish.

We ate quietly, the dark harbor and the dim lights on the docks providing a focal point for our eyes and, perhaps, our silence.

When we had finished our food, I ordered three Irish coffees and pulled the MacBook out of my backpack. "I made some notes today," I said. "I created a timeline of events related to Kris Kramer's disappearance. You two help me think through this to see whether I've missed something obvious."

Moeller sipped his most recent Scotch. "I wasn't much help earlier, but I'll give it a shot."

"Whatever I can do," Sally murmured.

"Right," I said. "So. My first knowledge of this matter came a week ago Saturday, in the morning, when Don Kramer came down here and hired me to find Kris. I flew to Birmingham the next morning, checked into the Tutwiler, met with Kramer, and read some files on a case Kramer thought might be connected to his daughter's disappearance. The next morning I drove out to Kramer's house to meet his wife, Susan, and their son, Paul."

"But your timeline should begin earlier," Moeller said.

"I'm getting to that. Kris Kramer disappeared two days earlier, on Thursday, the nineteenth of January. Her roommate told me that her mother came to visit in the afternoon and left the campus with her for the start of a weekend at home. Paul Kramer told the FBI that he accompanied his mother to the campus. I don't know whether those plans changed for some reason. Maybe a family argument occurred; maybe not. I'm trying to remain objective here.

"At any rate, Kris did not show up for classes or practice the next day, and the campus security office contacted Don Kramer at his law office. Kris's suitemate mentioned that she also called Kramer's office when Kris didn't answer her cell phone. Don called home, and Mrs. Kramer told him she thought Kris had returned to school the evening before. Kramer called the Birmingham police department. The Birmingham police called the FBI when they decided they might have a kidnapping case.

"All that occurred on Friday, January twenty. The morning of the next day, Kramer borrowed a friend's plane and flew down here to speak with me."

"These versions of the disappearance aren't perfectly matched," Moeller observed.

"Yes. But neither are they perfect contradictions. They're just a bit muddled, as first-person narratives often are.

"Kramer's body was discovered in the rail yards in Birmingham late on the night of January twenty-third or early the next morning. We know now that he had been murdered that afternoon as he was leaving his office."

I heard a sharp intake of breath from Sally. "I didn't know that. When did you learn that?"

"Captain Grubbs shared some information about his investigation with me. I didn't mention it until now."

Sally heaved another quick breath and sipped her coffee. "Okay," she said.

"How was he killed?" Moeller asked.

"One shot to the back of the head with a nine-millimeter handgun," I told him.

"To continue with the chronology, when I interviewed Kris's roommate Akilah at school, she gave me a memory stick. She didn't know anything about its contents, and you and I, Hans, discovered that the contents were password-protected."

"And that, unfortunately, has so far been my only contribution," said Moeller. "If I had just had more time. . . ."

"It wouldn't have helped much. The contents are also encrypted, according to Michael Godchaux, the creator of the contents."

"And Godchaux is involved how?" asked Moeller.

I remembered my promise to Agent Alston and what I could and could not say about the informant. "Godchaux was also what's called a 'relator' – a whistleblower – in a *qui tam* case – sort of like a class action – Kramer was building against corrupt officials and others in Alabama. But I'm getting ahead of myself."

I sipped my Irish coffee and looked at the notes on the computer screen. "When I flew down here after Kramer's funeral, I discovered my boat had been searched and that someone had left a message on the old laptop I keep in the cabin."

"You didn't tell me about the message," Moeller said.

"No. I didn't think I should involve you to quite that level at the time."

"But now – so what was the message?"

"Something to the effect that I needed to stay out of the oil and gas business."

Sally looked from Moeller to me. "Surely that indicates that Kris's disappearance is somehow related to the lawsuit Kramer was working on."

"And that Godchaux and the information on that drive may hold keys to her disappearance," said Moeller. "Unless. . . ."

"Unless what?" I asked.

He shrugged. "There are at least two other possibilities. One is that the real kidnapper is conflating the kidnapping with the – what did you call it? – *qui tam* litigation in order to throw you and the FBI off the scent."

I smiled, looked down at my coffee, and took a little sip. At the moment neither Moeller nor Sally needed to know I hadn't exactly told the FBI about the message on the laptop. "And the other?" I asked.

"The other is that the message did come from the bad actors in the oil and gas case, but they had nothing to do with the kidnapping."

"How does Kramer's murder fit in?" I asked Moeller.

"Same analysis. Could be related to the kidnapping. Could be related to the *qui tam* case. Could be related to both."

"Or, just keeping it logical, maybe neither," I said.

He nodded. "Yes."

"Let me go on through the timeline," I said. "So after I returned to Birmingham, I spoke with Sally again to see if she could help me find Akilah. Sally took me to the suite she and Kris Kramer shared. . . ."

"And we discovered Akilah had been murdered," Sally said.

"Yes. Her room had been searched, and she had been strangled. It seems a strong possibility that it was someone who'd been sent to look for the thumb drive. My presumption has been that the intruder did not expect to find Akilah there and killed her to remove a witness."

"Pointing to some relationship with the Michael Godchaux business," Moeller observed.

"Right. The next day I spoke with Mrs. Kramer again, and she and I visited the Woolf White firm, where Bill Woolf created an arrangement for me that would allow me free rein to review their files on the Godchaux matter."

I skipped the dinner date and the overnight in Sally's condo. Although Moeller had never hesitated to describe the activities on the *Billy Tell* or in his chalet southeast of Geneva, I preferred a little mystery. And besides, at the moment Sally sat close enough to touch.

"The next morning a local talent named Billy Royal breaks into my hotel room posing as a room service waiter and tries to muscle me."

"And fails." Sally smiled a little.

"Later, Royal tells me he had nothing to do with the boat incident and that a guy who looked Italian hired him, but he doesn't know the guy's name."

"How plausible is that?" Moeller asked.

"I believe him. If you met Billy Royal you'd understand. He's not capable of making anything up.

"And that's essentially all the important events. This recitation hasn't been as linear as I'd have liked. Anyway, before speaking with Royal, I flew to New Orleans and met with Godchaux. Godchaux gave me the password for the thumb drive, and when I returned to Birmingham, I turned the thumb drive over to the FBI so they could extract the files."

Moeller finished his most recent Scotch and noticed, apparently for the first time, the Irish coffee. "Did I order this?" he asked.

"No, Hans, I ordered one for each of us," I reminded him.

"Thanks, my friend, but I can't drink coffee late at night. Keeps me awake, you know. I need my sleep in order to keep up with the young ladies," he said. "Single malt Scotch, now, that's different. Quite different. Good for a body. Anything interesting on the thumb drive?"

"I haven't heard from the fibbies yet. I handed over the drive this morning after meeting Royal at the jail."

Moeller nodded. "So how close are you to finding this girl and solving a murder?"

I shrugged. "Solving the murder of my client is not my job, not technically anyway. The police and FBI are on it. They have a few leads. But my best guess, and probably theirs, is that the killer was probably sent by the same people who hired Billy Royal, and that the murder is related to the oil and gas investigation."

Moeller persisted. "And the girl?"

"If it's a kidnapping case, it's an unusual one. No ransom note. No contact from anyone who claims to have taken her. Most of the time in such cases those circumstances are not good news."

"Why?" The question was Sally's.

I glanced from Moeller to Sally and back. A bit of cream and a tablespoon of coffee remained in the bottom of my glass. I drank it off before answering and set the glass down with a louder thud than I intended. Flying back to Birmingham was definitely out of the question until the middle of the morning. "Because most of the time if there is no ransom note within two days, the victim doesn't make it out alive."

Moeller finished his Scotch. "Well, Slate, you've managed to render me depressed, tired, and drunk. I shall have to repair to the quiet of my boat and process all this information in my sleep. Perhaps then some answer will come to me in my dreams."

"Answers would be welcomed, whatever their source, my friend."

Outside, Moeller made his slightly uncertain way toward the *Billy Tell*, while Sally and I carried our bags along the catwalks to slip A-7. The *Anna Grace* sat, gleaming softly in the dim electric light, graceful and undisturbed, in the calm still water of the harbor. I stepped onto the gunwale, gave Sally a hand up, unlocked the companionway door, and stepped aside for Sally. She stepped down the steep stairs carefully, then turned around with a big smile. "I've never spent the night on a boat. Two firsts for me today."

I smiled. "If you're lucky, maybe we can make it three."

CHAPTER TWENTY-SEVEN

Tuesday, January 31

A few minutes after six, I rolled out of the double berth, careful not to waken Sally, pulled on sweats and boat shoes, and went topside. There was no rain, and the temperature was in the high forties, but low clouds threatened and a damp breeze made the temperature seem lower. I walked over to the marina and bought two large styrofoam cups of marine-grade coffee and brought them back to the boat. A few others were stirring around the marina grounds, fishing crews, a few marina employees, a boat owner or two.

Sally was in the shower. I placed one of the coffee cups on the stainless sink ledge in the galley, went back topside, and sat with my feet in the boat's cockpit.

The day after I'd thrown everything in the Camry and driven south from Birmingham all the way to Beach Boulevard, the southernmost east-west road in Alabama, I'd driven over to the marina at Orange Beach – owned then by Fob James, a former Alabama governor – and bought a live-aboard sailboat. I renamed it the *Anna Grace*.

But the boat was more than a home. A thirty-two foot Allied Seawind ketch, she'd taken me solo around the Florida peninsula, through the Florida Straits and up to Bahia Mar, a pause for fresh water and provisions before the short sail over to Freeport. She had been south and east to the Caymans, south to Jamaica and down to the Leeward Islands. Constructed of fiberglass, she was strong and solid and, because of her ketch rigging, easy to sail single-handed. One of her predecessor sister boats was the first fiberglass vessel to circle the watery part of the world. She was fast, too; she'd averaged a hundred miles a day on the run to Jamaica.

The *Anna Grace* and slip A-7, Orange Beach Marina, Orange Beach, Alabama, had been my home now longer than any other place I'd lived as an adult.

At this hour in the winter months, the marina was quiet enough to hear water lapping gently against the unmoving pilings, punctuated by the occasional squeak of a boat rubbing against a bumper or the musical clank of rigging slapping a mast. Not yet visible over the Florida panhandle, the morning sun painted the eastern sky orange.

The companionway door opened. Sally climbed the stairs carrying the styrofoam coffee container in one hand, the other holding closed an old robe of mine. She sat beside me in the cockpit.

"Good morning," I said.

"Hey," she said. "I think I like sleeping on a boat."

"Once you get accustomed to the new sounds, the slight motion is a little like being rocked in a cradle."

"Something like that, I guess."

We sat for a few minutes in silence listening to the sounds of the marina morning: a few low voices, the cries of seagulls, and in the distance, a heavy diesel engine snorting to life.

"Did we accomplish anything last night?" Sally asked.

"Oh, I'd say so."

She elbowed me. "Besides that. Did the discussion at dinner help?"

I shrugged. "No conclusions. But the exercise did crystallize the events for me and helped me get the timeline straight."

"That's something," she said.

"Yep." I swallowed the last of my coffee. "We need to start back."

"I'll get dressed." Sally stood, gathered the robe at her waist, and stepped with care out of the cockpit and down the companionway.

North of Gulf Shores, almost at the Baldwin County line, tall electrical transmission towers and power lines require a brisk initial climb of all aircraft heading north from Jack Edwards airport. No problem for the Albatros, but my practice has always been to peg the airspeed at best angle of climb, V_x, the speed at which maximum altitude is gained per unit of ground distance. Even in a single-engine Cessna, especially when the air is cold and dense, this airspeed yields a deck angle that can create the illusion that the airplane is going straight up. In the Albatros, the angle is even nearer vertical.

This time I left Sally's headset volume turned up, and this time she didn't scream on takeoff. All I heard was a quiet "wow," as the wheels came up and I pulled the nose up to peg the airspeed. In minutes, we had leveled out at ten thousand feet, and we cruised into Birmingham with only a minor traffic delay for sequencing and landing.

Back at Sally's condo, Sally changed clothes and hurried out the door to return to her office. I chose a blue blazer, white shirt, and repp stripe tie. It was time to update Bill Woolf on the status of things, including my meetings with Michael Godchaux and with Agents Sanders and Alston.

CHAPTER TWENTY-EIGHT

Sally texted me just as I was knotting my tie. "MY OFFICE NOW!"

Then, almost immediately, another. "CALL ON YOUR WAY."

So I locked the door, walked to my car, and headed toward the Alabama Southern campus.

Once in the car, I chose Sally from my contacts list and selected her phone number. My call went straight to voice mail. I didn't leave a message. The campus was minutes away, and she would see that I had called.

At the campus gate, the same guard I'd seen before waved me through. Before the bar came down behind me, my phone rang. "Slate," Sally said. "It's Paul Kramer. He's here, in my office. I already called Captain Grubbs, and he's here too. Paul says he knows where Kris is."

"I'm thirty seconds away. Thanks."

Leon Grubbs and Chief Miller were both standing in Sally's inner office. Paul Kramer, looking pale and miserable, his hair unwashed, sat on Sally's couch. Sally sat near him, her hand on his shoulder. Grubbs, Miller, and Sally were speaking quietly to the boy.

Paul Kramer shook his head in answer to a question I could not hear. "Nobody ever looked in the secret room," he said. "Not the FBI, not the police. Nobody. And my parents didn't tell them to. My dad never goes —never went down there, and my mom, well, I guess she didn't want them in there. I don't know." He shook his head again and stared down at the floor. "I should have told someone before, I know."

Miller spoke. "What about your mom not wanting the police in the secret room? What do you mean?"

Paul Kramer shook his head again and let out an explosive breath. "Don't you see? It's my mom. She's kept Kris down there all this time. She wouldn't let her come out. She's . . . she has her locked in there. My mom has my sister locked up in our house."

Sally looked up at me for the first time, her expression a mask. Grubbs noticed me and said, "I think we're about to find your missing girl." He pulled his cell phone out of his pocket, made a call and barked orders at the person who answered.

"Who could know?" Sally said to no one in particular.

"I wanted to tell someone. My mom forbade me to tell. Dad didn't know. I don't know why she did it," he was saying.

Grubbs said, "It's all right now, son. We're going to get your sister out of there."

Paul looked up at Grubbs and Miller, then noticed me. "My mom?" he said.

"One step at a time, Paul," I said. "First let's allow the police to do their jobs and make your sister safe. Then we will see about what to do regarding your mom." I looked at Grubbs. "Mind if I tag along?" I said.

"Right behind me," he said.

Miller said, "We will stay right here with the boy."

"I'll stay with you, Paul," Sally said.

"Let's go," Grubbs said.

The immediate vicinity of the Kramer home was a chaos of black and whites and unmarked police cars, parked at all angles, half in the street and half on the lawn. The TV film crews were in hyperdrive, reporters and their makeup people and cameramen elbowing each other for space to shoot standups. They shouted questions at Grubbs as we picked our way through the police cars, but he shook his head and grunted out "No comment." Wet trees dripped rainwater onto my shoulders as we walked through the Kramer front yard and into the house.

Inside, Agent Patricia Sanders sat at the booth in the kitchen across from a tall blonde girl whom I recognized from her pictures: Kristina Kramer. They were both drinking tea. The girl wore an Alabama Southern sweatsuit, and her feet were bare. In the girl's lap, I noticed a small stuffed deer, tan with white spots. Two fingers of one hand rested on the deer's head. Across the island from them, wearing a priest's collar and looking uncomfortable, stood a slim middle-aged man with dark hair and a graying goatee.

Agent Sanders looked up as Grubbs and I walked in. "Library," she said, inclining her head. We walked down the hall and found Bill Alston and four uniformed police officers, two wearing Mountain Brook police livery, the others City of Birmingham. The cops were having a discussion about jurisdiction. They stood flanking an expressionless Susan Kramer, who sat on the red couch wearing a beige pantsuit of a nubby material that might have been raw silk. Her makeup flawless, her wrists and neck encircled with gold, gold loops with green stones in her ears, she might have been waiting for a table at the Mountain Brook Country Club.

Grubbs solved the cops' jurisdiction issue. "We're in the city of Mountain Brook. Officers, this city has jurisdiction. I'd suggest that you exercise that jurisdiction and take this woman down to the jail."

"And charge her with what?" asked one of the Mountain Brook cops, a balding heavy guy, sweating even in wintertime under his bulletproof vest and uniform. "Being an overprotective mother?"

"Unlawful imprisonment in the second degree, violation of Alabama Code Section thirteen A dash six dash forty-two, restraining another person of the age of eighteen or older. A class C misdemeanor in Alabama." Grubbs turned to me. "Miss Kramer is eighteen, isn't she?"

"She's nineteen," I said.

"Well, there you go," Grubbs nodded at the officer. "What are you waiting for?"

"I have to hear from my chief," the officer said. "I'm not arresting someone in these circumstances without his okay."

"Give me your radio," Grubbs said.

The Mountain Brook officer unclipped his handheld radio from its place on his belt and passed it to Grubbs.

Grubbs spoke into the radio for thirty seconds, then passed the radio to the officer.

The officer listened for fifteen seconds, then, "Yes, sir," the officer said. "Yes sir, we're bringing her in now."

He turned to the other Mountain Brook officer. "Drive the car around to the garage. We'll take her out through the back." He took two steps over to Susan Kramer. "Mrs. Kramer, stand, please," he said. "Hold out your hands."

Susan Kramer obeyed the orders without a change of expression. The officer placed the cuffs over her wrists and snapped them closed. "Mrs. Kramer, you are under arrest," he said.

While the policeman recited the *Miranda* warning, he and Grubbs escorted Susan Kramer down the hall, bypassing the kitchen, where Agent Sanders and Kris Kramer remained huddled over their tea, and took her out the door leading to the home's attached garage.

Catching Agent Sanders' eye, I raised my eyebrows in a question. In answer she shrugged slightly. I walked up and introduced myself to Kris Kramer.

"Hello," she said, extending her hand. "Kristina Kramer."

"Yes, I know. Lots of folks have been looking for you."

The young woman shrugged. "I know. Sorry to cause trouble. Ms. Sanders has explained a little of it to me."

"I'm just happy to see that you're safe," I said.

"Where were they taking my mother?"

"Your mother . . . has some questions to answer. The Mountain Brook officers are taking her to the Mountain Brook jail."

"Jail? My mother hasn't done anything wrong."

Agent Sanders looked over at me. She raised her eyebrows and mouthed "Stockholm?"

I spoke again to Kris Kramer. "I'm sure this will all get sorted out."

She nodded. "With my mother it will. But my father's dead. Agent Sanders just told me."

"I know. I'm sorry."

"How did he die?" The question seemed directed to both of us.

Agent Sanders leaned over the table and extended a hand toward Kris Kramer. The girl's hands remained in her lap, the fingers on the head of the stuffed deer moving seemingly on their own volition. "I'm afraid he was . . . killed," Agent Sanders told her.

"Killed how? An accident?"

"No. Kris, he was murdered."

"Oh." The fingers on the stuffed animal stopped their movement. "Who?"

"We don't know yet," Agent Sanders said. "But we're all working to find out."

"Maybe it doesn't matter," Kris Kramer told her. "Where is my brother?"

"He's with Coach Kronenberg," I told her.

"Good," she said. "He'll be safe there." She looked up at me. "Tell him I'm okay, would you?"

"I will," I said. "I'd best be going now. It was nice to meet you, Kris."

"Same here," she said.

In the foyer I ran into Agent Alston. "So, what happened here?" I asked.

"We all made mistakes," he said. "You. Me. My partner. Local cops. Maybe even your client Don Kramer."

"Not looking behind the family's story, assuming that what seems obvious is also the truth, accepting the conclusions of the group. I could name several more. But how?"

"Turns out that the house has a secret room in the basement. You absolutely cannot see it if you don't know it's there. The basement appears to be a perfect rectangle, but another basement room, completely underground, juts out toward the street. That front wall of the basement is paneled in such a way that one of the panels is actually a door. I walked all through the house alone the night Don Kramer called us in, and I never saw it."

"But Kramer knew it was there."

"Sure. But from what I understand, the family rarely used that room. Off-season clothing storage, an old safe, old toys, some odds and ends. Nothing much, really. The first owner of the house constructed the room to serve as a storm shelter. Solid walls. Even soundproof.

"The family entered the room so rarely the Kramer woman even left the boy alone in the house. Finally, though, he suspected his sister was there but apparently couldn't confront his mother. So he called someone from Alabama Southern, maybe one of his sister's teammates, hitched a ride out to the campus, and told his sister's soccer coach that he thought his mother had his sister hidden away."

"Why?"

"Why did she do it? How? What? When? Where? I'm good at answering those questions. Or at least, usually I'm pretty good, or I wouldn't have the badge in my pocket. Why? For that you need someone at a higher pay grade." He shrugged. "But apparently it's got something to do with needing attention. I've been on the phone with one of our shrinks. Excuse me. Forensic psychologists. He mentioned a mental disorder call Munchausen Syndrome by Proxy.

"This thing that happened to the Kramer woman – it isn't quite that. That's where a parent, usually the mother, fakes the kid's illness because the parent craves attention. Here the Kramer woman faked the kidnapping, maybe for the same reasons that drive people with this Munchausen Syndrome. The psychologist is on his way down here from Washington. Thinks it's an interesting case, he says, unusual in the literature but not unique. Thinks it's also somewhat analogous to certain cases of child snatching by the non-custodial parent."

"Needing attention," I said.

"Yep. Something like that, sport. Why?"

"Nothing," I said, but I was thinking of Kramer and Sally. "So who's going to take care of these kids?" I asked Alston.

"We're working on it," he said. "A neighbor with children their age spoke with a Mountain Brook officer and me a few minutes ago out on the sidewalk. She will be taken into the house through the garden and the rear entrance. She seems capable and willing."

"Good," I said. "I'd just as soon not have anyone do something stupid like calling the Department of Human Resources."

"Makes two of us, sport. In any event, the young lady in there is over the age of majority."

"Right. Later, Alston."

Outside, Leon Grubbs stood in front of a swarm of handheld news microphones, cameras, and recorders. The cameras wore plastic hoods to protect them from the steady mist. The looks in the eyes of the scribes said Grubbs would be occupied for awhile. I saluted in his general direction, got into my car and drove away. Not one member of the media showed me the slightest interest. Maybe I needed to work out more often.

Back at Sally's office, someone had scrounged a mug of hot chocolate mix for Paul Kramer. Sally gestured for me to follow her to her outer office. She stood facing me only a foot or so away, her arms folded across her chest. "He's now aware that his sister is physically unharmed and in reasonably good spirits and that his mother is not in the house. He seems to be settling down. But someone needs to find a competent counselor for the Kramer children," she said. "They were not the sort of family to keep a psychiatric practice on speed dial."

"No. But as it happens, I do," I said. "I know some good people. I'll see what I can put together on short or emergency notice."

Sally went inside, and I used my iPhone to call Dr. Bev Adams' office. It was two in the afternoon, and Bev happened to be between appointments. I described the situation, and she promised to send a crisis counseling team from the UAB psychiatry department to the Kramer house. "Promise me, though, one thing, Bev: no state agencies," I said.

"I work for a state agency," she pointed out.

"Yes, but you're different. You know what I'm saying. No Alabama do-gooder bureaucrats. Back when I practiced full time, I did some *pro bono* work in juvenile court. I've seen kids taken away from loving parents who were trying the best they could and not abusing the kids at all. I saw some appalling things."

"I understand," she said. "Bad things happen even when good intentions abound."

"Especially when some of those good intentions are exercised by state agents with unlimited power in their little worlds."

"Slate, I don't disagree. But let me be practical for a second. Aren't the children now in two locations? We don't have the staffing power for that."

"I'm about to deal with that," I said. "Both will be at the home in Mountain Brook by the time your people arrive."

I stepped back into Sally's office. Paul Kramer was finishing his hot chocolate. "Listen, Paul," I said. "Your sister is with some members of law enforcement at your home, and I understand a neighbor with kids your age may be there. She wanted you to know that she's okay. Wouldn't you like to be with Kris now?"

He looked up at me. "Yes," he said. "I'd like that a lot. Could someone take me there?"

"I'll drive you," Sally said.

"We'll both go," Miller said. "Take my school car. Official visit."

"Let's go," Sally said to Paul.

Sally, Chief Miller, and Paul Kramer left the office together as I tagged along behind. Sally locked her office door, and we walked together down to the building's lobby.

"My car is parked in back," Miller said.

"I'll call you," Sally said to me.

"I'll be around," I told her.

The three of them headed toward the rear exit of the sports complex, Paul Kramer between Miller and Sally. Miller had a hand on the boy's shoulder. I watched them for a moment, then turned and made my way out.

CHAPTER TWENTY-NINE

Outside, the weather had not improved. Students scurried across soggy school quadrangles, eyes half shut, heads bent against the cold mist, the reds and blues and yellows of their rain gear blurring to gray in the filtered winter light.

My work on the matter of Kris Kramer was done. More accurately, it was over, since I had done nothing to lead to the girl's return to her family. But then, neither had the FBI, or Leon Grubbs, or Bill Woolf, or, indeed, her own father. What was more, her father's theory of the reason for her disappearance, a theory that I and every law enforcement agency had adopted as our own, had been disproved by the facts. In the course of looking into that theory, I'd managed to stir a nest of hornets and set them buzzing into my face, despite the fact that these particular hornets had, as to the matter at hand, been minding their own business. My client had been killed, execution style, almost certainly by a professional hired by the organized crime interests at the center of the investigation

Michael Godchaux had instigated when he'd walked into the office of the United States attorney in New Orleans. And a young woman with a promising future had died, no doubt for the same reason.

In the car, I started the engine and, idling in my visitor's space in front of the athletic complex, called Woolf White and asked for Bill Woolf. Though I was certain the news of Kris Kramer's reappearance and her mother's arrest had spread throughout the law firm by now, I thought I had a certain duty to speak with him.

But he wasn't in. I left a message with his legal assistant letting him know I wouldn't be back in the office and that I would return the firm's files and arrange for the FBI's return of the thumb drive to someone at the law firm. I put the car in reverse, drove slowly out of the parking lot, down the access road and through the automatic exit gate, and left the Alabama Southern campus behind. Having nowhere else to go, I drove back to Sally's condo, let myself in, and changed into workout clothes.

Shoeless, I dragged my cushions out to the middle of Sally's living room and just sat for fifteen minutes. Every meditator from the most advanced practitioner to the beginner experiences monkey mind, but today my mental monkey jabbered and skittered from tree to tree and threw bananas and coconuts at me for ten minutes until I wrestled him to the ground. For the last five minutes, focusing on the breath, I just watched thoughts arise and allowed them to pass away.

Then I pulled on my running shoes and a hooded rain jacket and jogged twice around the perimeter of the Highland Park golf course. About halfway around the second time, it occurred to me that I had skipped lunch.

Back at Sally's condo I showered and changed. When I powered up my iPhone, I had a text from Sally: "On way home." I texted back "Here now. Early supper Bottega?" After a minute, she answered "Sure. "It's close."

Kristina Kramer had turned up safe and sound, but I didn't feel much like a victory celebration. Susan Kramer's mental illness, the unspoken possibility that Sally's relationship with Don Kramer may have fueled in

Susan Kramer an emotional crisis that resulted in — what to call it? — the sequestration of her daughter in order to try to gain attention.

After we ordered, winter lettuces and risotto with veal cheeks and artichokes for Sally, crab cakes and guinea hen with pancetta, cipollini onions, polenta and red wine for me, Sally said, "We're both quiet, considering."

"We are," I agreed. "Sometimes words fail in the face of human complexity." We'd been seated promptly on a slow afternoon in a front corner seat in the two-story neoclassic building, the glass of the window at our elbows soaring all the way to the twenty-foot ceiling.

"Something you don't know," Sally said. "After everyone left my office this afternoon, I met with Akilah Ziyenga's parents. They were here to claim their daughter's body and fly back home with it." She brushed her hair back behind one ear. "And I'm thinking about resigning as soccer coach at Southern."

I considered a response while I watched the commuters go by on the wet pavement of Highland Avenue. "Well," I said finally. "I think the team needs you right now."

She nodded. "Thanks for saying that. But I'm not so sure. Maybe a new coach, fresh ideas, new approach, would help them put all this behind them. Not sure they don't somehow, some of them, blame me for Akilah."

"Did the parents say anything?"

"No. They could not have been more gracious in the circumstances. No, but some of the girls, well, I don't know, they know who found her, maybe think I had some involvement, even if it was peripheral, in the matters you were working on. It wouldn't surprise me if some of them transferred. So I thought, maybe I should go back to Chicago, maybe coach high school soccer again."

"Hmm. I never asked, but, did any of them know about you and Don Kramer?"

She frowned. "Not the time to talk about that. Thought we wouldn't. Ever. But no. No one knew. Not for sure. I suppose a close group of young women might notice things."

"Like a jury, collectively, misses nothing."

She put down her fork and glared at me. "A jury? What we did wasn't a crime."

"No, of course not. It's just a lawyer's analogy. Collectively, juries don't miss anything. Similarly, maybe a women's soccer team wouldn't miss much either."

She sighed. "Maybe silence was better. Let's just finish dinner."

In the condo, I made two cups of hot tea, and we sat together on Sally's couch gazing at the lights on Red Mountain. After some time, Sally asked, "You remember when you told me about meditation and Buddhism?"

"Yes."

"You never asked me about my religious views."

"No, but I think I was headed out the door then."

"Maybe. Anyway. I grew up Catholic. But I'm a very lapsed Catholic. Not really a believer anymore. At all."

I sipped my tea. "Neither I nor most Buddhists would have a problem with that. No deity in Buddhism. Buddhism teaches what to do, not what to think. It's a practice. A mental discipline."

She nodded slowly. After a few minutes, I said, "I think we're both tired from the last couple of days. I'm getting sleepy." I carried my teacup to the sink and rinsed it and returned and sat cross-legged on the floor facing the couch. "My work here in Birmingham is done," I said.

"I know." Sally shrugged. "You did your best."

We sat in those positions for a few more minutes without speaking, then Sally carried her teacup to the kitchen. "I'm getting a bath and turning in early," she said.

While Sally was in the shower, I prepared for the night as well. I slept fitfully but must have finally drifted into a deeper sleep, early morning, because when I awoke around six, Sally was already gone. She'd left a note on the counter, saying to leave the key in a kitchen drawer if I was leaving today and to let her know I'd arrived safely back home. I showered, dressed, packed, left the key where Sally wanted it, and let myself out.

CHAPTER THIRTY

Wednesday February 1

Boats at rest, like automobiles undriven, suffer from the effects of entropy at an accelerated rate. The only maintenance-free boat is the one you don't own. Various inventions slow the decay: heaters, pumps, dehumidifiers, paint, caulk, epoxy, varnish. Winter maintenance for a boat that stays in the water requires running the engine once a week or, preferably, taking the boat out for a short cruise.

For me the challenge was nowhere near as daunting as for the weekend or occasional sailor. The *Anna Grace* was my home, and maintenance on my boat did not also require commuting to the marina, chasing supplies, reinventing relationships with marina employees, and a thousand other time-wasters the part-time sailors had to endure.

Below about thirty-nine degrees, the interior of a boat can frost over, creating even worse moisture problems than boats suffer from without frost. So when I'm away, I leave a little ceramic heater and dehumidifier running full time in the cabin to keep the temperature above the frost level and keep down the humidity. Maybe ten years old, the device had come with the boat. While I was away, the heater had malfunctioned, died, and tripped the ground fault circuit.

I fired up the big propane heater I used for a heat source away from the dock to bring the temperature up quickly and dry some of the condensation. I packed up all the cabin bedding, damp from the humidity and on the verge of mildewing, in a couple of heavy black trash bags and carried it to the marina's laundromat. I left the bedding with the attendant after asking her to run the loads with hot water and a little bleach. I'd do my own clothing later.

Back at the boat, I spent the better part of an hour wiping down the interior, trying to get rid of all the excess moisture. Then I drove to Home Depot and bought a tiny ceramic heater and the smallest dehumidifier they had. I installed them in the cabin, checked out the electrical circuits, and got them running.

Then I locked up and walked over to the marina restaurant for lunch. Green salad, then gumbo with crackers. I considered a beer, then iced tea, but defaulted to hot tea. Too cold for anything refrigerated or iced after a morning spent in a damp, cold boat cabin.

After lunch I picked up the bedding, fresh, dry, and warm, from the Hispanic laundry attendant and left her too big a tip. I made up the berths in the cabin of the *Anna Grace*, now a balmy sixty-eight degrees and pleasantly dry, lay down in the V-berth and started rereading Michael Dibdin's *Dead Lagoon*. I was tired, though, and the warmth of the cabin and the rocking motion of the boat soon put me to sleep.

I was dreaming of jogging along a tropical beach with palm trees that grew almost down to the water, when my iPhone jolted me awake and I struck my head a glancing blow on the slanting bulkhead next to the berth in the boat's bow. For a minute I couldn't locate the iPhone until I remembered I'd left it in my shirt pocket. I dug out the phone on perhaps the fourth ring. "Yeah," I said.

"Slate." Both the voice and caller ID told me it was Leon Grubbs.

"Yep. You got him."

"Slate. Grubbs. Listen, uh, Slate, remember I told you the FBI was running the stills from the security video at Park Plaza through their facial recognition software?"

I sat up and swung my feet to the floor. "Yes. I remember."

"Well, I just received the FBI's report. They have a match."

I stood and crab-walked aft. I had to stoop to avoid the low ceiling. "That's good. Are they sure?"

"Yes. They're sure. And I'm sure. We have a suspect under surveillance and will probably make an arrest today. Slate, I need you to come up here so I can go over the report with you."

"Why? What do you need me for? You haven't asked for my approval for the thousand and one other arrests you've made. Arrest the guy."

Grubbs' voice was flat and even. "Not the point, Slate. This is information I need to deliver in person. You need to come up. Today. Now."

"You're serious." It was both a statement and a question.

"You know I am."

I stuck my head out of the companionway. The sun was out. "Okay. I'll see you this afternoon."

"Call me when you get here. I'll be waiting."

I arrived at the offices of the Birmingham Homicide Division shortly after three and walked straight into Leon Grubbs' office. I knocked and walked in uninvited. A couple of officers, a lieutenant and a sergeant, were standing in the office. Grubbs, seated at his desk, spoke to them in a low voice. He stopped as I entered. "Slate," he said. "I didn't think you'd be here this soon, but I'm glad you are. You were at the coast, were you not?"

He turned to the two officers. "That's all for now, guys, and thank you," he said. "Close the door on your way out."

Turning to me, Grubbs said, "Sit down, Slate." He picked up a folder from his desk. "Move your chair closer so we can both see this report."

I pulled up my chair, and he turned the folder sideways and opened it. "This is my reading copy, not the official file." The cover page of the report was printed with the legend "FBI – Confidential." Grubbs turned the cover page. "I'll show you the entire report and explain the methodology behind it if you need me to, but I'll spare the suspense. Slate, this is not going to be easy, but here it is. The person in the stills from the video at Park Plaza has been identified by the FBI's facial recognition program."

I suppressed a sense of dread. "Right." I shrugged. "You told me that on the phone."

Grubbs nodded. "The person identified is the women's soccer coach at Alabama Southern. Sarah Kronenberg. Also known as Sally."

I stared down at the report, uncomprehending. After maybe thirty seconds, I said, "It's a trial program. Obviously it makes mistakes."

"Believe it or not, that was my first thought as well. But I was on the phone for an hour with one of the men at the FBI who worked on the development of the NGI program. He explained that the software is actually now more accurate at recognizing faces than human beings are.

"Thing is, normally the FBI uses only the mug shot database. The software reviews that database in a few seconds, they say. When that came up with no match, I asked them if they could expand the search to other databases, military records, lawyers, other people whose fingerprints and identification photos have been taken.

"Like you said, it's a pilot program. NGI. Next Generation Identification. FBI gave the stills to some state agencies that participate in the pilot. Illinois State Police got a match from an Illinois database of high school coaches. Sarah Kronenberg. Coached high school soccer in Oak Park, Illinois, ninety-seven through ninety-nine."

"It has to be a mistake."

Grubbs looked up at me and shook his head. "I'm sorry, Slate. We arrested her this afternoon after I called you. She's already signed a confession. It's not a mistake. Sally Kronenberg killed Don Kramer."

I shook my head and flipped through each page of the report. The print had begun to blur, forcing me to concentrate; the report explained the methodology of the facial recognition software and ended with a printout from the Illinois database that included a photograph.

I looked closely. Though she was years younger, there was no doubt. It was Sally.

I looked back at Grubbs. "Okay. Thanks. Thanks for doing this in person. I appreciate it."

I stood and looked at Grubbs for a moment. "The body was moved," I said.

Grubbs nodded. "I understand what you're thinking. But she's young, and she's an athlete. She's strong enough." He appeared to want to say something but stopped himself.

I turned, groped for the doorknob, found it, then turned back. "The soccer player," I said. "Akilah Ziyenga. What about her?"

Grubbs shook his head. "We don't know. Still working it. But for what it's worth, we know it wasn't Ms. Kronenberg. She was with other people continuously around the time of death."

"So you looked at it that way too?"

Grubbs just turned both palms up and nodded. I turned to the door and a few seconds later found myself standing on the First Avenue North sidewalk.

I started walking. Down to Twentieth Street, then south. South past Morris Avenue and the railroad district not far from where Don Kramer's body had been found. Further south toward UAB and the area called Five Points. Where Sally and I had dinner that first night. But before I started up the hill toward Five Points, I turned right along Seventh Street and realized where my unconscious mind had been taking me. Smolian. The psychiatric clinic. Bev Adams.

I rode up the old elevator, its cables rocking the car back and forth gently. A family of three rode along. The man seemed defiant, the woman resolute, their son, of perhaps fourteen, sullen. When the doors opened, I walked to the registration desk and told Renee I needed to see Dr. Adams.

"Mr. Slate, how good to see you," Renee said. "But, did you have an appointment today?"

"No," I said. "I need to see her now, please."

"Well, she is pretty busy today, so I'm not sure if you can see her. . . ."

"She'll see me," I said. I walked around the partition that separated the reception area from the waiting room and headed down the hall toward Dr. Adams' office. Just as I started, I saw Bev Adams' door open, and a man in a white coat with a stethoscope around his neck emerged from her office, turning for some last remark as Bev Adams stood leaning against the door jamb. Dr. Adams saw me out of the corner of her eye and broke off her conversation. "We'll have to finish this later," she said to the other doctor.

She turned to me. "Slate!" she said. "Is it about the Kramer family? We have a couple of crisis counselors working with those children."

"Sort of," I said. "May I come in? It will just be a minute."

She caught my expression and frowned. "Of course." She held the door for me. I sat in one of her client chairs, and she closed the door and went to sit at her desk. "What is it?" she asked.

I reached down and unstrapped the little Ruger from my ankle, pulled it from the holster, popped out the magazine, ejected the round from the chamber, replaced the magazine, pushed the gun back into the holster, and laid the holster with the gun inside on Bev Adams' desk. Then I took off my coat, unsnapped the Bianchi shoulder holster, and went through the same operation with the big Glock. I put the coat back on before I spoke.

"You told me not long ago that if I felt suicidal, you would want me to give you my guns. Here they are."

"Slate." She shook her head once sharply. "I'll find a place to keep your guns if you want me to. But obviously this means you aren't feeling well. What's happened?"

I told her, sparing no details.

When I had finished, she said, "I see. Will you go to see her?"

I had thought about that a little on my walk. "At some point, probably yes. But not right now."

"You should remember that this relationship was a tentative step back into close relationships. You should also realize that the way it ended is no reflection on you. This happened. But it happened only once."

I nodded. "Thanks."

She gestured toward the guns. "Is there any likelihood that you could be tempted to harm yourself through some other instrumentality?"

I'd thought about that too. I shook my head. "No. Not a chance."

"All right." She stood. "I will keep these until you ask for them back. And I'll give them back if your reasons for wanting them back are the right ones. Now I have other patients to see." She came around the desk and gave me a quick but firm embrace. "Call if you need me."

"I will," I told her.

I saw myself out.

CHAPTER THIRTY-ONE

I'd meant what I'd said to Bev Adams. No other means of harming myself other than one of those guns would ever occur to me. Aircraft, for example, should not serve as anyone's instrument of personal destruction. Disliking my life enough to harbor thoughts of ending it was no reason to destroy a machine as fine as the Albatros.

Flying lore teaches that in addition to preflighting your aircraft, you should preflight yourself. No doubt every flight instructor in the world would have advised me against flying back to the coast. But they weren't me, and they wouldn't understand. I needed to spend the night on the *Anna Grace*, not in some hotel. I had a perfectly fine airplane sitting on the ramp, and that airplane would get me back to Gulf Shores in thirty minutes. Once the preflight started, the pilot – I – would become a technical-minded stranger with my hands. Detachment. Compartmentalization. These brothers would serve as my co-pilots for this flight.

I walked back to First Avenue North, retrieved the car I'd borrowed at the FBO, drove to the airport, preflighted, taxied out and took off.

I was sitting at my desk in the Lost Lagoon Lounge with a tumbler full of ice and Maker's Mark, my first but probably not my last. I wasn't quite ready to head back to the marina and begin this solitary night.

The days were lengthening in lower Alabama. Reds and purples streaked across the western sky out past the Fort Morgan peninsula and Mobile Bay to the west, the sun a point or two below the horizon but still providing enough light to see out past the sandbar to the open Gulf.

A late-fishing pelican skimmed the surf, its head swiveling in a desultory search for supper, the coming evening darkening the water underneath the pelican's wings, the wind blowing the water white and black. Sandpipers made their usual mad rushes at the foamy edge of the surf. Over across the jetty on the lighted stage at the Pink Pony Pub, a couple of blonde girl singers in flowing white dresses appeared to be warming up, but the wind snatched away the sound. I did not think that they would sing to me.

ACKNOWLEDGEMENTS

I would like to express my gratitude to my family: Janet Hill Gregory, my wife, reader, editor, and supporter; and Sam Gregory, my son, reader, assistant editor, and cover designer.

Grateful acknowledgement is made to the following for permission to reprint previously-published material:
Everett Eaves, author, AAPG Special Volumes, Volume M 24: North American Oil and Gas Fields, AAPG (1976). Reprinted by permission of the AAPG, whose permission is required for further use.

223

ABOUT THE AUTHOR

Steven P. Gregory earned B.A., M.F.A., and J.D. degrees from the University of Alabama. Gregory has practiced law since 1991, concentrating on complex litigation and alternative dispute resolution. He lives in Birmingham, Alabama, where he is working on *Spring Thaw*, the sequel to *Cold Winter Rain*.

www.ingramcontent.com/pod-product-compliance
Lightning Source LLC
Chambersburg PA
CBHW051241250626
47155CB00009B/3123